No Man Will Know

and other stories

Donald Southey

I0611682

WIPF & STOCK · Eugene, Oregon

Wipf and Stock Publishers
199 W 8th Ave, Suite 3
Eugene, OR 97401

No Man Will Know
And Other Short Stories
By Southey, Donald
Copyright©2017 Apostolos
ISBN 13: 978-1-5326-6988-0
Publication date 9/23/2018
Previously published by Apostolos, 2017

Contents

Acknowledgements

I particularly wish to record my thanks to Mathew Bartlett and the team at Apostolos, for their interest in my stories, which quickly turned into enthusiasm, and all their help through the publishing process.

Thanks are due also to my wife and daughters, as well as several fellow-members of Freedom Church, for their consistent support and encouragement. This collection of stories would not have seen the light of day without you.

I confess to having shamelessly raided friends, colleagues and relations for many personal names and surnames. I hope you will take it as a compliment, and not read anything into the characters who have stolen your identity!

Bible quotations on pages 60, 82, 88–91 are from the New International Version, (c) 1973 - 1984, International Bible Society (British edition). One quotation on page 90 is from New English Bible, first edition 1961, copyright Oxford University Press/Cambridge University Press.

Prohibition

Introduction

This story is set in the very near future, and started from a question, "What if ...?"

A few years ago, there was news of a disease that affected bananas. It was feared that the virus might spread quickly through all the Caribbean islands and Central America, and no cure had yet been found. (However, after some months, it seemed the problem was not as bad as it was feared.)

At the same time, there were many "Health scares" in the news. Every month, there was another story that some food or drink or drug was harmful. European governments were also passing many laws to protect public health. For example, some food colours, preservatives, and also insecticides, that had been used for many years, were no longer permitted. People were grumbling about this constant "interference", saying that the public should be able to choose to be healthy or not.

This story supposes two things. Firstly, that the banana virus did wipe out most of the banana crops of the world; only a substitute (called "Plantainillo") was immune. Secondly, that the governments of the USA, UK and European Union had banned, for public health reasons, a very popular drink ...

Prohibition

The clouds were spaced out as if they had been sown in drills; rows of little irregular puffy lumps, taller than they were wide, and spaced not-quite-evenly down the line of the wind. They were also a lot nearer than they had been. The plane was evidently losing height. You could tell that without even looking at the little map on the plasma screen. According to that, they were at 28,500 feet altitude (why did America still persist in using non-metric units?) with an outside air temperature of -18°C, 0°F, had passed the Belo Horizonte transmitter some time ago, and were approaching the one at Campinhas.

The cabin crew were starting down the aisles, handing out leaflets. He knew the drill by now; there would be four altogether, two for immigration (one for everyone, one for foreigners), one from the ministry of health, one from customs.

"Travellers from the European Union and the United States of America should take notice that some products of Brasil are not permitted to be exported without licence from their own

Government and from the Brasilian Ministry of Agriculture. These include;

- Monkeys, dogs, cats and all mammals

- Peroquets and all live birds

- Reptiles, fish, live insects and spiders

- Skins and furs of any animal or taxidermy specimens

- Coral and other marine product of living origin

- Embryonic material, human sperm or eggs, whether or not viable

- Viable plant material from uncertified source

- Guns, weapons, swords and knives more than 6"(150mm) blade

- Ammunition and fireworks

- Drugs and medications from uncertified source

- Coffee, and caffeine derivatives of any sort."

He nudged his daughter awake. "They're coming round with the landing forms," he said as soon as she had one eye open.

"Mmmph," she replied, stirring out of her sweaty nest, blinking and then extending a limp hand to take a set of leaflets. She screwed up her eyes to focus on them for a moment, then slid back under the rumpled blanket.

"Don't settle down again, you need to fill those in. We're only half an hour from São Paolo."

He always chose a window seat if he could, fascinated by every change of view. You could see more detail of the ground below now. There was still a lot of scrub, but more and more of the land was evidently cultivated. Even from up here, the fields looked big; huge quadrilaterals of subtly different colours. The bright terracotta of the soil often showed through a thin covering of even green. Here and there a vivid red road cut a straight ribbon between tiny homesteads, or a curious formation like a crop-circle showed where a giant irrigator was used to water some high-return crop. Some of the patches that looked like scrubland or forest would in fact be plantainilloes; Brasil had led the way in finding a substitute for bananas, and still exported eighty percent of the world's supply, although the Caribbean and

Central American nations were starting to catch up now.

What was missing of course, were the huge fields of row upon row of coffee bushes, which used to look like giant green ploughed fields from this altitude. Although ... actually, that field there ... it *might* just be one. After all, it was still legal to drink it here.

He sighed, and started to fill in the paperwork. The two immigration forms asked for almost exactly the same information, and had to be filled in with black ballpoint pen, as if anyone used those now, horrible leaky things. But then, this was Brasil; incredibly modern in some ways, backward in others, and bureaucratic to a fault.

At least his daughters could all write as well as they could type; he'd made sure they practiced. And when Katie, the eldest, had landed this voluntary work opportunity in Central Brazil, she'd really thanked him for it, and even e-mailed her sisters saying, "Whatever you do at school, DON'T stop real writing on real paper!" Out here, ninety percent of everything had to be done on paper, as ninety percent plus of people –

especially in the poor districts – had no e-access at all, even now.

"Where are we staying – do you know?" he asked.
"With Katie, of course," yawned Debbie.
"Yes, but do you know the address?"
"Somewhere in Karaiba. That's Minas Gerais ... It's Setor Sul, oh, Bàrrio Jardim something."
"Any street name?"
"Yeh, oh, whatsit, Rua Presidente ... Presidente Anthony Garotinho. Dunno the number."
"So they're naming streets after him already, are they?"
"Yup. Katie says he's even more popular now than Lula was."

He filled it in on both his forms, leaving spaces.
"Oh, yeh, I just remembered. Edificio Ayrton Senna, 23."
He looked at the forms. On one he could just fit it in; the other had boxes. Bother. He tried:
ED . A . SENNA23 – just possible, without a space. He continued;
RUA PRES . A . GAROTINHO
B . JARDIM a few spaces;
SETOR SUL, KARAIBA / MG

An annunciator tone, *bing-bong*, made him look up; the seatbelt warning was not on; it had only been the information screen. Something labelled IMPORTANT had overridden the flight map.

"Oh, look, Dad, it's how to fill the forms in. That's cool."

"So it is. Oh – pants. I've done this one wrong. Arrhh!!"

"Ice down, Dad. They won't get arsey about it."

"Sweetheart – please don't use that word."

A sigh. "All right – they *won't mind*. That better?"

———

São Paolo Guarulhos airport was still grey, drab, and full of milling people. Each time he'd come it had seemed slightly more crowded. Again they had a walk of what seemed like a kilometre before they came down the stairs into the Immigration hall and the snaking queue for "Non-Brasilian Passports". Mercifully it was less than a hundred long.

"We must have hit it right for once."

"You mean it's usually worse than this?" Debbie looked tired just thinking about it.

"I've joined it back on the stairs before now.

There, look behind you."

Hard on the heels of their planeload were another Superjumbo-full of travellers, looking aghast at the queue that was now almost filling the rope zigzag.

"You'd think they'd have found a better way by now."

"They have, for nationals. Biometrics coded onto their passports."

"But don't ours have that?"

"Yes; but the systems, or the coding, is incompatible. Foreigners still have to queue and wait."

"That," sighed Debbie in her most grown-up voice, "is ridiculous."

They found the correct conveyor belt after several attempts, collected their luggage, loaded a cart ("This is *mediaeval*," muttered Debbie) and pushed it through the green channel to emerge on the concourse.

The echoed sound of the crowd filled the high hall, varied by snatches of passing conversations, a crying baby, the staccato rattle of the destination boards.

Something irresistibly drew his eyes to the right, to the little cluster of shops and food outlets. It was several moments before he realized why; it was that half-forgotten aroma –

"Dad?"

"Mmm?"

"Do you want to stop? Have something to eat?"

"Aah ... no ... No, let's not. I'll only want a drink."

"Well, you can, you know."

"No ... I mustn't. I'll only start wanting it again."

"So?"

"So, we're only here for a week and a bit, and then we go home."

She shrugged. "OK. Let's find the bus."

Pushing the luggage cart out of the terminal building, the damp evening warmth settled on him like a cloak. The traffic hubbub and the street lights reproached the sunset and the darkening sky. And the smell – the indescribable layered aroma of a subtropical city; damp dust, steaming earth, hot tarmac, diesel and tyres, gutters, the scent of a huge flowering shrub, a faint underlay of sewage, all told him unmistakably that he was back in Brasil.

The bus was one of the things Brasil did best. Air-conditioned luxury, seats that reclined more than any aircraft ones (bar first class maybe), rapid, cheap – and best of all, direct to nearly any city within four hundred miles, from a terminal right next to the airport.

He paid by plastic, the driver loaded their cases and gave them the claim stubs, Debbie picked the seats, and they settled down to a ten-hour trip. "We'll actually get there faster than flying," he remarked, as the door eventually hissed shut. "That's 'cos you have to change airports, and the next flight is tomorrow anyway, isn't it?" "Yes, and we'd have to stay in a hotel, and so on." "Great. Wake me up when we get there. Iced water's in the armrest thing." She dropped the reclining seat and cocooned herself in a blanket, wriggling around like a hamster.

———

He watched the absurd mix of buildings and structures that was São Paolo slip past, a never-ending stream in the gathering dusk; modern highways, seedy motels, decayed colonial houses jostling with concrete boxes and glass corporate HQs. On and on, past a Byzantine railway station, palm-lined avenues, bridges, underpasses, tower blocks, dredgers on the river, construction sites and huge hoardings; between all these, neighbourhood shops, bars, bus shelters almost hidden under fly-posters, hectares of little block-houses with tin roofs – and away from the centre, on almost every inch of spare land, shanties and squatters' shacks, under bridges, on waste tips, even on a new road under construction.

"Dad?"

"Not asleep yet, sweetheart?"

"No ... I'm thirsty."

He found a beaker of iced water and pulled the rip tab for her.

"Thanks ... that's better. Dad; is coffee really addictive?"

What a time of night to be starting a serious conversation.

"Well. No, addictive isn't a fair word. It's habit forming, for sure. I smelt it in the airport and I really wanted some. And of course I haven't touched it for three years. But it's not addictive like a lot of drugs; where your body or brain chemistry alters and you need to have it. Like nicotine. It's just not in the same class."

"What about the health dangers?"

"Well, I may be biased, as an ex-coffee drinker; but I think they've been highly overplayed, to justify the law. Heart disease – I don't remember any doctor of ours saying that coffee was the biggest cause, or even a big cause, of heart disease. If you have a tendency to that, then coffee won't help you, it'll contribute to it, I guess. Kidney failure – I suppose there may have been a few cases that were all down to coffee, and again, if you had problems, coffee might make you worse. But I think a lot of it has been hype; scare tactics, really."

"What about people going hyper when they were wired?"

"That – well, I don't know. We used to drink an awful lot of coffee in college, and I don't remember any of us doing anything stupid. I think the problem was really those high-caffeine drinks for clubbers, in the early 2000's, especially if you combined them with some other stuff. People on Club 18-30 holidays, showing off to their mates – there were some horrific things happened there. But whether it was anything to do with coffee, I doubt very much."

"What about road accidents?"

"Oh, that's one of the craziest ones of all. Do you know, up to just a year or two before the ban, the motoring organisations – and even the police – were encouraging people to take caffeine drinks when they drove? Helps concentration, and improves reaction time, they said. Medically proven, they said. Have a break and a coffee every two hours or two hundred kilometres, they said. The RAC even had a high-caffeine drink branded for them, put their name on it. No, the "evidence" all suddenly appeared out of nowhere, over a few months. Before that, no-one had ever been heard to say that coffee contributed to road accidents."

"So why did they ban it?"

"I really don't know. I think it became a Cause, really, a few people getting hold of an idea and shouting very loudly about it, and touching all kinds of nerves like public health and safety. Then it started to become "politically correct" – you remember that phrase? The thing to my mind is, it's so inconsistent. If caffeine is the culprit, why include decaffeinated coffee? And why allow tea? Yes, even strong tea has less then half the active ingredient, but it's still the same stuff, near enough. But anyway, you shouldn't be listening to my views, because I'm biased."

"Well, so are they. No-one's allowed to say different. That's stupid." She was silent for a while, listening to the faint drone and hiss of the bus. "I like talking to you, Dad, you know such a lot." She snuggled back down with her head against his shoulder. "Thanks for bringing me."

"That's OK, pet. You're welcome."

The bus was climbing into the hills now, with the vast sprawl of São Paolo finally slipping away behind them. It was almost night. The only things you could see out of the window were the road, the jagged western horizon, stars, the occasional lights of oncoming traffic or a roadside building, and silhouettes of power poles and trees rushing by.

He made sure his wallet was safe, and settled down to sleep.

―――

He woke, partially, three or four times, in chilly echoing bus stations, dimly glaring with tired fluorescent lights. Finally his eyes told his brain that his dreamed recognition of the road into

Karaiba was, in fact, reality. He jerked awake. They were off the main highway and in the southern edge of the city. Over the river, around the next bend ...

"Wake up, sweetheart. We're here."

The bus circled the terminus almost completely before zooming into the entrance, as if it wanted to take it by surprise. They stopped with a hiss and a bounce rather than a jerk. Debbie finally got her eyes open enough to gather her things and stumble out of the bus. They collected their luggage, and with all their hands full looked around, trying to collect their wits.

"This way."

The bus station was a drab concrete shell, brightened by advertisements and little shops, kiosks really, selling beer, Guaranà, hot dogs, pão de queijo, postcards, sweets, cigarettes, and just about everything else. They walked out past the ten or so different ticket offices and the taxi firms' desks to the main doors.

"Are we early?"
"No, I don't think so; I made us right on time."
"There she is, Dad! KATIEEE!!!"

17

Two huge hugs later;

"Well! How are you? How's the project? How's-"

"I'm great! How's Mum? How was your journey? Are you guys tired? Do you want to eat?"

"Mum's fine. It's so good to see you. And yeah, breakfast would be great. We last ate on the plane. Didn't bother at S.P."

They walked across the damp car park, already steaming where the early sun was slanting through the acacias, an old nut-brown beggar eyeing them from under the shade.

"I'll take you back to Flávia's. She'll love to see you. Hey, do you like the car?"

"Hey! Nice wheels. And yellow! you always wanted yellow ... Looks good. You got this with the money we sent?"

"From the church? Yup, I only had to pay the insurance out of my own money. Paolo found it."

They loaded the case and squeezed in. "Does it cost much to run?"

"Nope. Wood alcohol. No acceleration, but who cares? it gets me around. I went to Brasília in it last weekend. And I've not even needed to put oil in yet."

Flávia was waiting as they clattered in to the tiled lobby of the apartment block.

"Aah! Steeven!" she cried. "Is so good to see you! an' this is Debbee?" Hugs, kisses. "Come, come; your bags, I take them, we have café da manhá, yes? You are hungry?" She pulled out the first syllable of the word, making it into *haaangri*.

"Yes," he smiled, "we are hungry. Thank you."

Flávia's flat was cool and dim after the glare outside. There were fresh rolls, every bit as good as in France; pão de queijo, like cheesy brioche buns; ham, cheese, butter in a tin, chocolate spread, guava jam, honey, hot milk, papayas, mangoes, plantainilloes, salt crackers, and over it all ...

He suddenly realised that Flávia hadn't stopped to ask him what he wanted to drink. And café da manhá meant, of course, 'coffee of the morning' ... he'd better say something.

Too late. She had poured him a large cup of steaming, black, strong coffee, and was piling in spoon after spoon of sugar. The aroma was almost bringing tears to his eyes. He hadn't smelt a drink that good in what, three, four years?

She caught his look from the corner of her eye. "Ohh ... I don't ask. You have sugar in coffee?"

"Er — we don't have coffee, now, in England ..."

"Oh, but here, in Brasil, of course you have coffee. Mmm?" Katie was saying something to her in Portuguese. "Ahh, yes ... I give you café con leite. Is milk, not so much coffee. Is OK for you."

It was hot milk with a large dash of expresso, like the 'latte' they had served in all the coffee franchises in the early 2000's. He couldn't refuse, not that he wanted to. Every fibre of him yearned at that moment for wonderful, milky, sweet Brasilian coffee, that variety they grew here that had almost no acidity but full, exquisite flavour. As he put the cup to his lips and breathed in that long- remembered, long-forbidden smell, he suddenly wondered if he was wrong about coffee not being actually addictive ...

Even that little amount brought a small giddy rush of blood to the back of his head. He was really going to have to be careful. He forced himself to stop gulping and attend to the food instead.

"Dad, are these real bananas?" Debbie was asking.

"No, I don't think so. They're plantainilloes, aren't they?"

Katie nodded. "They call them bird-bananas here. They've bred a slightly bigger sort now, they're in the markets here but I don't think you can get them back in Europe yet."

"Yes, I thought they were bigger. They're sweeter, too."

"That's because they leave them to ripen on the tree, they don't cut them green and send them across in a refrigerator, like for Britain."

He picked one up and peeled it. It was a little bigger than the usual English ones; as long as his middle finger, rather than his index. The smell was delicate, slightly floral. He bit into it. Debbie was right, these were sweeter; and the texture was better – really almost like a banana.

"They'd love these at home," he remarked.

"Well, they'll get something even better soon," replied Katie.

"What do you mean? Have they cracked the virus?"

"No, not quite. Don't hold your breath, it's a few years off; but they're reintroducing real banana plants into a couple of isolated areas – where there's been no trace of disease for over five years."

"Really? How will they keep them disease-free?"

"Well, they're well away from any other growing areas, and I think they are disinfecting vehicles that come, that sort of thing. Like I say, they're just trying it out. Have you met Paolo's father?"

"Don't think so."

"He owns this farm, somewhere way upstate, and they use it for breaks. He's signed up for the scheme. All sorts of things he tries out there, 'cos it's a hobby rather than a business. I wonder ..." She turned to Flávia and asked something. They chatted away for a couple of minutes.

"Flá says, Paolo's Mum and Dad are going up there next weekend. I'm going to see if Paolo can get us invited. Oh, don't look awkward, they love having people out there. Paolo likes showing the place off, I think. You'll love it, they've got horses to ride, and all sorts. Leave it to me."

———

The Project was no more than two kilometres away.

"It's just SO good having my own car now," called out Katie, as she drove with both windows open and the air-cooled engine growling like a tiger in a tunnel. "This used to take me an hour each way on the bus, and it wasn't even safe. And it was just hopeless relying on lifts – you know what Brazilians are like. It meant I couldn't promise anyone I'd be there, or get anything regular going."

"Do you mean, like classes?"

"Like anything. Especially a class. If you, the teacher, don't turn up one week, three-quarters of the class don't turn up the week after – and most don't bother to come back at all."

"So what classes have you started now?"

"English – that's Improver's English, next step after what they did at school – and I.T. for beginners. You wouldn't believe how many of these kids have never sat in front of a computer. And they'll never get a job, except like collecting rubbish, without any basic I.T. skills."

"Don't the primary schools at least give them keyboard training?"

"Not round here. You have to go to a posh school for that, a middle-class one where you pay. It's absurd; the State can't even shell out for a dozen computers per school. Never mind the Net."

"You're right. That is absurd. Brasil is leading Europe in some of this stuff, these days. I'd have thought every school would have had broadband by now."

"Yeah. They should have. President Garotinho started a scheme to do it nationally. But half the States decided they couldn't pay for any basic computers to connect to. [Get your own side of the road, porco!] So they said, we'll save up for the hardware, and just quietly pocketed the money."

"What!! Literally? I thought Garotinho was cracking down on corruption."

"Yes; at the top, nationally, he really has been. The trouble is, there's all these layers of government: federal, state, region, city, district ... It's not filtered down everywhere yet. Makes me mad, but what do you do? Here we are."

They stepped out into the Third World.

Even the rubbish at the sides of the streets had been picked over for anything you could build or waterproof a shack with, or eat. The bare red earth showed through the bones of the street. Opposite, a jumble of bits of wood, plastic and wire showed where someone was trying to fence off their little plot to grow some sad-looking vegetables in front of a breezeblock coalshed, their house. It was the best-looking dwelling on the street. Only the "church" was any better; the walls were straight, and whitewashed.

The meeting hall was about the size of a double garage, and filled with cheap plastic chairs. Someone had painted crude bright murals inside. There was a table at the front and a microphone stand, but no P.A. or music keyboard. Nothing else at all, in fact.

"They bring the sound system along on Sundays, so it doesn't get nicked," said Katie. "The odd chair is always going missing, but they're cheap, and it's not the end of the world. So far, no-one's trashed or nicked our cars because we help them – they know we wouldn't come back if they did that. I've got a big black guy in my English class who offered to be my minder. I said God was my minder, but I'll give him a Real each class night if no-one breaks into my car. It's worked."

They went through to the back. There was a compact, canteen-scale kitchen, very Spartan but basically well-equipped. There was one more room, half the size of the first. A middle-aged man was bending over looking at the floor, every inch of which appeared to be covered in vegetables.

"This is Pastor Henrique," said Katie, pronouncing it *En-hee-kee*. At his name, the man straightened up and turned to offer a grubby hand and a huge smile. Katie finished the introductions, and several more sentences before turning back.

"He's very sorry he doesn't know any English," she said. "He's the pastor in charge here. He runs the prison visiting, and the food aid, and all sorts. I'm helping organise the classes; we have a catering chef now, who teaches cooking, home economics and food hygiene, three days a week – the other three days she does the same on the other side of the city. And there's another lady who does baby care and basic pre-natal stuff."

"All this – is this the food aid?"

"This is part of it." Katie was slipping in and out of Portuguese to Henrique, between the English sentences. "This is soup. They have a soup run every Thursday and Saturday night. Henrique has contacts in the big market, and gets offered lots of stuff that's just going past its best, and they can't sell to the shops. They add a small sack of beans, and there you are. Different soup every week! ... He and Anna, that's the chef, will cook all this up today, starting after lunch. This week, he's got enough to do Monday night as well, he thinks. They gave out nearly three hundred portions last week, word has really got round."

"Three hundred? Just vegetables?"

"Yes, dad," said Katie quietly. "Don't know we're born, really, do we?"

———

"You hold the classes here in the meeting hall, do you?"

"Yes. Mostly in the evenings, because quite a few people work in the day."

"How do you do the I.T.? Have the church in town funded some kit?"

"Yes. There's a lovely guy there – you've met him – Pelé, named after the footballer, and he's a whiz with computers. He's built me a system where ten keyboards can all link into one foldup – what you still keep calling a laptop, Dad – which can run them all, and relay back to ten little six-line displays, off old cash tills. It's so immac.

Everyone can see what they've just typed, and it's only cost as much as two foldups – about three-K reaïs."

"Less than a thousand Euros? That's very good. And you can teach ten people at once?"

Katie gave him one of her looks. "Twenty, Dad. This is Brasil, you share a keyboard."

"I stand corrected. Brilliant. – Are you still enjoying it?"

A glow, rather than a mere smile, spread across her face. " I love it."

She looked more beautiful than he could remember her, leaning on that rickety old table in front of three dozen plastic chairs in a tin-roofed garage, dressed in scruffy clothes, quietly enthused with helping twenty strangers get a better job.

This isn't just for another year, he thought. She's found her calling.

———

He was pleasantly surprised by the red road. He had expected bone-shaking potholes, and a fifteen-kilometre-an-hour crawl; his heart had sunk when they told him it was fifty kilometres off the hard-top highway.

In fact they were going to make it in a little over an hour. Just as well, after driving for five hours already. And two stops for the children.

Katie was following Paolo's car, making a very respectable speed, and switching sides of the road now and again to avoid the worst gulleys. It was wide enough for three lanes, had there been any traffic. The surface was packed hard clay, surprisingly flat, and slippery when wet. Fortunately the rain had stopped before lunch. Even though the road was not dry yet, the little yellow car was slowly turning orange in Paolo's dust trail. "I daren't use my wipers", she remarked, "it'll smear to mud and I won't see a thing. I'll stop and wipe the windscreen in another ten k's or so."

Clearing the windscreen twice en route, they rolled into the fazenda late in the afternoon. Everyone peeled themselves out of damp car seats, and the two children ran to meet Granny. Like everywhere in Brasil, the one-storey farmstead was built for coolness and shade, and was so dim it took several seconds to adjust your eyes, coming in out of the sun.

Paolo's father knew almost no English at all, and his mother very little, but they were most welcoming and easy to get on with. Granny brought out cakes and coffee; "Have this now," said Paolo, "we will have dinner later, maybe an hour."

Steve was suddenly nervous. "Paolo, is it all right if I have a soft drink? Fruit juice maybe?"

————

In a little while, the ladies all took the children off to hose them down, while the men sat around the huge, heavy table and talked. The crude wood stove glowed and hissed, and beans slowly bubbled in an enormous pan. The maid quietly pottered at the sink and the range. An antique and rusty chest freezer was graced with a lacy tablecloth and a vase of flowers.

"What do you grow on the farm?"
Paolo had to translate.
"We grow all sorts. Our money, we make from cattle. But many things we grow besides. Cane, not for sugar, but for *pinga*. You know *pinga?* it is alcohol from sugar ... Rum? Yes, like rum. We sell, two reaïs for a litre. It's very good, the – how do you say? – the experts, they prefer it is made

on the *fazenda* and not in a factory. Also, they like very much this sort we make."

"Sounds like farm-made cider back home – but only two reaïs a litre? That's wild!!"

"Well, there is not tax like in Europe. – And some soya, and corn, a little, and coffee – and of course – now the bananas."

"I was going to ask about those."

"Yes, we are a long way from a traditional area for bananas, but the land is good here, and we get water from the São Francesco river. So my father says, 'Yes, I will be an experiment, bring bananas and I will plant them …' Ah, you should have seen it. The men from the Government in white suits like astronauts, all the tests they must do; three times they come before they are ready. My father says he thinks they just want to taste his *pinga* again ... Then comes the truck, like a big refrigerator, and everything must be washed with chemicals; the outside of the truck, the road, the gates. And so now we grow bananas. Not many, about one-tenth hectare. The Government, they send men each month, and they put on white suits, and cut little pieces to take away and test, like on the films when there is somebody killed, you know?" Grandpa was laughing at the standing joke. "Every month," continued Paolo, "my father asks them, 'Do you know yet who did it?' And the men smile, and drink some *pinga*, and take all the little bags away."

Before long, the sun was slipping down behind the huge mango trees, and the rusty whirring of the *cigarras* seemed to be louder than ever. They strolled outside to soak up the peace. Beyond the mangoes, the land sloped down to a broad floodplain, with the glint of the river – not much more than a stream at the moment – threading between brick-red banks. A kilometre away, real forest crowded down to the water's edge. The late light was heavy and golden in the air between them and the far shore.

"This is a lovely place," murmured Steve.

"Tomorrow, we will see the farm," said Paolo. "Relax now. There is plenty of time."

———

They set out, not too early, after breakfast. Granny didn't come; she bagged the children and was delighted at the prospect of amusing them for a few hours.

Coarse grass scratched at their ankles as they headed for the horizon.

"We only see a little bit of the *fazenda*, now," said Paolo. "Maybe more this afternoon. You can ride a horse, would you like this?"

They passed a small herd of curious cattle – most with humps, like Indian ones – and arrived at a field protected by two rows of trees.

Not surprisingly, the field was very big indeed. Unexpectedly, it was full of small, spindly, twiggy plants. The largest was about the size of a young blackcurrant bush. Fully half of them were no more than a single stem with leaves, about knee high.

Row upon row upon row of them, like a huge plant nursery, right over the hill.

"Whatever is this?" asked Steve.

"OK. Here we grow coffee; but not to sell the – the beans. We are not in a coffee area here, so there are not any workers with experience. We just grow and sell the little plants, for other farms to buy and grow the coffee."

"Now that does surprise me. Is there really a demand for that? I thought most coffee farms had gone out of business, and the few that were left had cut right back."

"Yes; until last year that is true. But this is for the future. My father does not think the law will last very long. When it changes – then he will make big money, for one year, two years. It is an investment. Like also the bananas."

"Paolo," said Debbie, who was losing her shyness, " do you suppose your dad would show us the bananas? I've never seen a banana growing. Do they really hang upwards?"

"My dad says, No problem. This way."

They turned and trekked along the edge of the coffee field, past a stand of maize and another of giant grass, that turned out to be sugar cane, and came to a kind of stile over a fence.

"The mat here, stand your shoes on it," said Paolo, pointing to a flattened mass of straw. "It's antiseptic. If you want to touch the bananas, wipe your hands on it also, like this."

They all did as they were directed. It certainly smelt like antiseptic.

"Watch out for snakes," warned Paolo.

They were now walking through an astounding variety of scrub. Occasional blackened tree-stumps showed that this had been cleared by burning, once at least. But the forest was coming back, although very little of it was more than two metres high yet. Fleshy-leaved shrubs and giant herbs jostled with thorns and little palms; low twisted trees spread small canopies; grass dotted with spindly flowers was tufting between everything, and only on the path could you see more than a glimpse of the vivid, almost fluorescent red-orange earth.

"This is a barrier," said Paolo. "We grow nothing here, and we keep out the cows."

It was hard to really appreciate it when you had to keep both eyes scanning the ground for snakes. They saw it in glimpses, a thousand different disjointed views, a strange beauty, a mixture of harshness and lushness; every so often the whoop, cluck or trill of some bird, and all the time a thousand crickets and grasshoppers in chorus.

The sun was becoming fierce and they were glad of the bits of shade on the path, when suddenly they arrived at another fence, with a massive confused wall of greenery behind it.

"Here we are."

They walked across a second mat of straw and stepped over a stile, into an organised jungle. Stems like beech trees, only softer, were topped with crowns of gigantic, ribbed leaves, like torn triangular quilts, every now and then stirring and fluttering like flags.

"All these have grown this year. About seven, eight months, no more."

The size of the things took your breath away; not one leaf was within reach, and each was two metres long. It was a forest of temporary trees, trunks that made a dull note when you knocked on them, but with no wood or bark to be seen.

"It's awesome," breathed Debbie.

"Huge, aren't they?" murmured Katie.

"It's almost like being on a film set; but they're *real*."

"Yes, laughed Paolo, overhearing. "They're real. See, I prove it. Come here, here."

There in the next row of the jungle, high over their heads, was a sight they had never seen except on film. A stalk, emerging somehow from the crown of one of these huge herbs, covered with strange green fingers, polydactyl hands cupping toward the sky, three or four circles of them stacked up around the central stalk. A few fingers near the top were actually half-yellow.

"It's soon ready," said Paolo.

He left them staring up at the phenomenon and drew his father aside for a moment.

It was a pretty spooky sensation, and Steve could only think of one thing to compare it with – standing in Rouffignac caves, underneath the painted ceiling, looking directly at, *breathing* on, pieces of art twenty thousand years old.

He sampled the moment with bated breath. Here they were, looking at some of the *first* bananas man had seen in years – a fruit brought back from the very edge of extinction.

He looked around. Where were Paolo and his father?

There was a thunking sound, like a mallet, coming from somewhere close by – on the edge of the little plantation, it seemed. Then a curious, moist creaking, with a falling pitch. Like ... like separating celery, or ... A huge rush of falling vegetation, leaves tearing, and a soft ponderous crash accompanied a sudden brightening at the end of one of the green alleyways.

They ran towards it. "Paolo! Are you there? Are you all right?"

They emerged, squinting in the sunshine, to see Paolo and his father standing triumphantly over a fallen giant of the jungle.

"Paolo! ... You *cut it down?*"

"Yes. It's the way to get them." Obviously relishing the moment, he slowly moved a leaf to reveal a smaller, yellower version of the cluster they had just been staring at.

"Would you like a banana?"

"Paolo!!! You ... The men from the Government – what will they say?"

"It's OK. They only say to my father, Do not sell them, or take them off the farm; your family can eat them. You are welcome."

"But ..."

"No, really, it's OK. My father says so."

"Dad," said Debbie. "I'd love a banana."

The topmost ones were just ripe. Paolo handed Debbie one, then Katie. Katie remembered how to peel them, Debbie needed to see how she started. They took their first bites.

"Ohh ..." mumbled Katie, shutting her eyes. "I'd almost forgotten."

"It's so different," said Debbie, swallowing. "Oh, Paolo, this is fantastic."

Paolo handed them round to the others. They ate one each, without saying another word. The rest of the bunch went over Grandpa's shoulder to take back to the farmhouse.

"Just don't tell anyone," requested Paolo. "Or we will have a thousand visitors!"

They retraced their steps through the cerrado, hardly speaking; indeed, hardly wanting to swallow and lose the lingering flavour.

———

"My father says, did you see the newspaper," said Paolo, passing it across the table, over the remains of a huge cooked lunch.

It was a week-old copy of one of the regional dailies, with pictures of the coffee ban protests from the previous month; the one in Washington, and the one in Berlin that had turned into a riot.

"You see, it will not last for ever," said Paolo.
"Maybe not this year, or next year, but soon, they will change the law. My father is sure of it."
"Well, your father has a lot of faith in democracy, I can see. Maybe he's right. I don't know."
Debbie was leaning her chin on his arm, poring over the text. After a few moments she put a hand out and took the corner of the page, as if to say "may I turn over?"
"I didn't know you read Portuguese."
"Mmmm ... only a little bit ... Did you see this, Katie?"
He left them looking at the paper and stepped outside onto the porch, where Paolo was fixing up a hammock.
"Do you like to sit in this? It's very relaxing. Here, please."
"Ah – no, thanks, I don't think I will; hammocks are wrong for my back. This chair is fine."
Paolo lay in the hammock himself, and swung gently, by means of one toe on the verandah.

"So, tell me about England, with no coffee. It must be hard, I think."
"Oh ... yes, well, I don't like having no coffee, it used to be a favourite for me. But you get used to

it. And we are allowed tea, of course."

"But tea is not the same."

"No, it isn't. But it's something ... Some people try and make their tea really strong, to try and get the same effect as coffee. I tried some once. It was awful, you couldn't drink it. So acrid."

"I heard that people smuggle it."

"Oh, yes, there's quite a little trade in bootleg coffee. But two things work against that. Firstly, there's nowhere we can take a car or a truck to, from England, that still grows coffee. This means that the smuggling isn't on a huge scale. Most of it is by air travellers hiding it in their clothes. And although people will pay quite a lot, it's not a narcotic, so you don't get people hooked – like with cocaine – until they will pay any price. This means that there is a high risk for not so much profit. Actually, there's a third thing, there's the smell. Even a sealed packet can be found by a police dog. And again, when you make coffee, it's almost impossible not to let any of the smell out of the room. In the end, someone will notice, and tell."

"Did you ever go to a house where they serve the coffee in secret? – It's all right," continued Paolo,

"I'm not going to tell the police! I am your brother!"

He shook his head. "No. Never have. We are very careful about the law, at least about not getting caught, in England. Me, I would never take the risk – I don't think a Christian should. Mind you, I nearly went into one by mistake once."

"How was that?"

"Oh, it was my work colleagues. We went out for a dinner one night, and they said, Let's go on to a bar. So we ..."

"You go to a bar? But you don't drink coffee?"

"Ah, no, that's not a bar like you have here; you came to England, do you remember pubs? More like that. I go to be a friend to my workmates, and I have cola, or juice, maybe one beer ..."

Paolo was shaking his head in disbelief.

"Yes, all right, it sounds crazy, I know. Yes, it's a crazy law. – But anyway; we went to one bar, and my friends didn't like it, so we left after one drink; and someone said, I know this great place near here. We all went along, and it looked like a club from outside, an OK one, only a bit quiet; the door was locked and my friend had to talk to someone through a little hatch to even get us into the first little lobby. Then these two big guys were patting him down in the doorway, and he whispers over his shoulder something about them serving "the real stuff" inside. My alarms went off, you know? and I asked him what he meant. He wouldn't say it out loud, but he made the word with his mouth, *coffee*. That's when I backed off, left them to it, and went home. I was looking over my shoulder for a good ten minutes in case any of the goons from that place were following me." Paolo lay back and laughed. "My God! It's like Chicago in the films."

"It wasn't funny at the time."

Katie had joined them. "What's this, Dad? Did you go to a coffee cellar?"

"No, I nearly did by mistake."

"It sounded like that one in Birmingham."

His jaw dropped. "How do you know about one in Birmingham?"

"Oh, my friends from college went there. They tried to get me in there, but I didn't want to. One of my friends had coffee at their eighteenth birthday party, pushing everyone to try it – remember that party last year, middle of May, when I phoned and asked you to collect me early?

And you thought I was bothered about the alcohol and what people were getting up to. Well, you were half right, but not about alcohol."

"You never told me about that."

"Didn't we? No, probably not." She smirked. "There's probably quite a lot we haven't told you about, isn't there, Debs?"

————

In Guarulhos airport, Steve lost Debbie for a moment. He turned back, and she was poring over a São Paolo newspaper in the rack at a magazine kiosk.

"Practising reading Portuguese again?" he remarked. "Bit late now, we're flying home in two hours."

"Mmm," she said, distracted. "Yeah – go on, Dad, join the queue, I'll be along in a sec."

She was nearly quarter of an hour. "Whatever were you up to, pet?"

"Oh, nothing, Dad. – Anyway, didn't Mum tell you that you never ask a lady that question?"

The flight home was uneventful, the one change of planes went without a hitch, and thirteen hours later they were disembarking for the last time, in England.

They collected their luggage and headed into Customs. Since the change in the law, you nearly always had to stop and speak to a Customs officer, even in the "green" channel.

"Good afternoon, sir, and where have you travelled from?"

"Oh, well, Central Brasil, with one change ..."

"Brought back anything in particular, sir? No livestock, plants, tobacco, any sort of medicines or drugs? ..."

"No, nothing but a few gifts – textiles, trinkets ..."

"Any coffee?"

"Oh, no. Of course not!"

"Ah. Just wondered if you'd be one of the first taking advantage."

He blinked.

"What?"

"I take it you've heard the news, sir?"

He shook his head. "What news?"

"They've repealed the prohibition, sir. Didn't you know? — And just back from Brazil, too, what a shame. Yes, you're allowed to bring back up to two kilos of ground or one kilo of instant, per trip, as from midnight last night. It'll be back in the shops from the end of the month ... So, no coffee to declare, then?"

"No ..."

"Actually –" Debbie was leaning around him – "Yes. A kilo each." She reached around and put two fat half-kilo bags of Brasil's best on top of his case. She grinned. "That's why you never ask a lady what she's been doing. Happy birthday, Dad."

No Man Will Know

Introduction

This is another story set in the very near future.

At present, in England, it is still possible for Christians to meet and pray and preach the gospel freely, anywhere; although there is constant pressure from politicians, the police, and local government to limit this.

Not many years ago, a law was nearly passed, that would have stopped Christians from freely teaching the word of God even in their own churches. It caused great protest. In the end it was defeated by just one vote, because Tony Blair had an appointment elsewhere.

We are told that such things are signs of the end times. However, there is a strong tendency among Christians to interpret what they read in Scripture to make a "whole picture" in their minds; then they strongly preach the interpretation, as if that were the Scripture.

This story is a caution against doctrine that makes us forget what Jesus really said about the end of the age, and what He did not say.

No Man Will Know

It began on the Friday night.

Little groups of believers all over the country were quietly getting together for the vigils that had lately become a tradition, since it was one of the few ways left of marking the second most important day in the Church's calendar. Even the former Free Church groups, who held lightly to such traditions, had started to do the same; it was becoming important to celebrate every difference, hold on to every connection that affirmed the identity of the family of believers. So many were effectively (though none officially) denied to them. Even the very term "Christian" had become such a term of abuse, through the years of misuse by the prominent, that it was avoided.

"Hello, Bob. Thanks for coming, and God bless you. Do come in."

"Hello, Dave; hello Marie. God bless you too. – Is Diana here?"

A frown. "No ... not yet. Nor's Maurice."

"H'mm. That's odd. They're usually the first ... It was seven-thirty, wasn't it?"

"Oh yes." Some things never seemed to change. If you wanted to catch Christians having a meeting, call just after seven-thirty. It was a miracle no-one had quite tumbled to it yet.

Mind you, by the time the door was answered, they would all have cups of tea and Social Action Society discussion notes ready.

Interruptions were mercifully rare, and there were none that night.

They got to their knees and thanked their God for their salvation, and the price He had paid on their behalf.

They prayed for the world, that largely despised them; for the government, that hemmed them in with petty rules; for their leaders, that had let them down so pitifully; for their society, ignoring the better way they offered and falling apart with discord and self-interest; for their neighbours, who ranged from suspicious to spiteful; and all without any apparent malice or even self-righteousness.

They broke up at half-ten, quietly feeling that they had been heard in heaven.

"That was a good evening, Dave, didn't you think so?"

"Yes; one of the better ones. Funny about Maurice, though."

"H'mm. And Diana ..."

Just then the phone rang. Marie answered it in the kitchen, and came back through looking shocked.

"It's Alison. She was phoning to ask if Maurice had left yet."

The room went silent.

"Did you tell her ... Is she still on the phone?"

Dave took the handset and stepped into the kitchen.

A minute later he came back in. "He left to come here at seven."

Everyone looked at each other.

After a moment, Marie said; "I'm phoning Diana. I know it's late ..."

There was no trace of either Diana or Maurice.

—

Bob was doing the Social Action Society accounts the following morning, and still wondering where the two regulars had got to, when Dave phoned.

"The police have been round," he said.

"What?" exclaimed Bob, as a familiar chill caught his heart.

"They found Diana's car, just round the corner

from us. They knew we were friends – through Social Action – and wanted to know if she had visited us last night."

"Do they know what happened, or where she is?"

"No, apparently not. I told them we'd had a SAS meeting, and that you could vouch for the fact that she wasn't there – I hope you don't mind."

"No, that's OK. I don't suppose you asked them about Maurice?"

"No."

"I'm sure they'd ask, if they were investigating."

"Yes."

"So let's hope he's turned up."

"And let's hope Diana does too."

"You're not – a suspect or anything, are you, Dave?"

"I don't think so. They didn't drop any hints like that."

"What a strange business."

"Yes. Look, keep in touch, won't you? If you hear anything else."

"Yes, sure."

———

Three hours later, Bob was indeed back in touch.

"Dave, you'd better sit down for this."

"What is it? Have they found ... one of them?"

"No."

Dave sat down. His eyes slowly got wider. Marie came in, and was about to ask an innocent question, when he signed for her to be quiet. She sat down with him until he hung up the phone. He was white.

"Whatever's the matter, love? You look like you've seen a ghost."

He swallowed. "Worse than that."

She took his hand. "What is it?"

He took a deep breath. "That was Bob."

"Yes, I gathered. What did he say? Was it about Diana, or Maurice?"

"Not exactly." He swallowed again. "He's been phoning round a few people. About, oh, tax relief on their giving, you know ..."

"Gift Aid."

"That's it. Well, another three people ... aren't there."

"What!! But – couldn't they just be out or something? Not answering the phone?"

"No; these are people who should be around and aren't – their partner, or children, or someone, hasn't seen or heard from them since yesterday, and is worried about them."

It was Marie's turn to go white.

"Another *three?*"

"And that's without counting any of the ones he can't contact. That's *at least* five missing people. All from SAS. It's – it's just not possible ..." His voice cracked.

They sat for a few moments, holding hands. A deep, unspeakable dread was slowly creeping over Marie. She thought she could see the same in Dave's eyes.

She had to cough before any words would come out.

"I'm going to phone round a few people," she quavered. Then, with more control in her voice; "To ask them to pray, you know?"

After about twenty minutes Dave silently joined her in the kitchen. She finished the phone call she was making and turned to him, ashen-faced.

"Oh Dave," she started, and then buried her face in his chest.

"Who?" was all he had to ask.

"Sean ... and James ... and Isobel," she gulped.
"That's another two," he replied in a whisper,
"Bob told me about Sean."
She looked up, tears filling her eyes. "And Uncle
George..."
"Uncle George too?"
She nodded. "*We've been left behind ...*"
And he clung to her, and she clung to him, and
wept uncontrollably.

—

"Come in, Dave." Bob was a different man. He
seemed to have aged ten years overnight; he was
moving with the weariness of the lately bereaved.
"Thanks ..."
"Will you have a coffee, or something stronger?"
"Stronger? Well ... I ..."
"Let me get you a sherry. I think we could both do
with one."
Neither of them normally touched alcohol except
for celebrations. Dave was too shell-shocked to
object, and found a small glass pressed into his
hand. They sat down.
"Pastor Turnbull has gone, too," remarked Bob.
"I've been making some more calls. Jim Stone,
from the Baptists, says two of his deacons and at

least three of his other people aren't contactable. I couldn't get hold of either of the Anglican vicars."

"Pastor Turnbull?" mused Dave. "We must have misjudged the guy after all."

No-one could remember Pastor Turnbull's first name, as he invariably preferred to be called by his title. His church was quite large and apparently thriving – as much as a church could thrive these days – and tended to take over, rather than support, any joint venture they approved of and entered. They were successful and they knew it; there was a distinct air of being the cream, emanating from Pastor Turnbull and permeating his whole flock. They were good folk, so it seemed harsh to label it pride; but everyone else came away feeling slightly second-class, resentful of it – and ashamed of their reaction.

"Well, if so, then I have to hold my hand up to misjudging the Anglicans. I'm sorry to say I never really rated either of them; I always thought of old Bill as weak, and the new fellow at St. Matthew's struck me as an intellectual with no heart for people. It sounds terrible to say it aloud, and so bluntly, but that's my confession."

At that moment there was the unmistakeable crash of glass, somewhere close by. Dave jumped to his feet, Bob only turned his head.

"That's not ours," he said after a moment.

"They're picking on old Gordon Bucket down the road these days. He reacts, you see – runs out and shouts at them."

Dave could hear shouting in the street, an adult roar and a piping taunt in reply.

"The ringleader, must be all of seven, and has an air rifle. The police can't touch him, can't even confiscate it." Bob sighed. "I'd hate to be a copper these days. Must be worse than being a believer."

They sat in silence for a moment.

"What do you make of it all?" asked Bob.

"Well ..." began Dave, and then couldn't continue.

"What does it look like to you?"

"Marie said ..." He shut his eyes for a moment, and forced the words out. "It's like we've been left behind."

"The Second Coming ... the Gathering–up of the Saints ... yes?"

"Yup." He buried his nose in his glass to hide his

emotions. The sweet heady smell and warming taste did at least distract him with its comfort for a moment.

"My first thoughts too," replied Bob.

Dave took a long moment to absorb the remark. "*First* thoughts?"

Bob stood up slowly and walked over to the window. "Yes," he answered. "It's what we've been taught to expect, since we were so high, but ..." He gestured at thigh height.

"But what?"

Bob turned around. "Too much doesn't fit."

"But ... what do you mean? What else can it be?" Saying it brought a renewed lump to Dave's throat.

"That's the trouble." Bob was coming more alive again. He began to pace. "I don't *know* what else it could be. But it still doesn't fit."

Dave looked completely baffled. He put his head in his hands. "Bob, don't kid yourself. Look, we know that we were never going to know all the details ..."

"Nor the day, nor the hour. Yes, I know all that. But there are *some* things we know. And the more I think about these, the more they don't fit."

"You're going to have to explain."

"All right." Bob was beginning to get animated. He started to use his hands as he talked. Dave found himself thinking how nice it was to have the old Bob back, as if he'd been ill or down for years, not hours. It felt like years since last night. "First, the passages in the Gospels. Doesn't Jesus say that all men will see him coming on a cloud with power and glory?"

"Yes; but isn't that after ..." He still couldn't quite finish the sentence.

"After the Rapture of the Saints? That's what we've assumed. But look again. Next verse in Luke: 'When these things begin to happen, lift up your heads, for your redemption is drawing near.'"

Dave was shaking his head. "That doesn't mean it has to happen *after* the Son of Man has been revealed."

"No, but it has to happen *at* that time. Doesn't Paul say that the dead in Christ will rise first, when he comes, and *then* we will all be caught up to meet him in the air?" He picked up a Bible, open on the desk, where he had evidently been working. "Here it is, in First Thessalonians ... and there's something a bit similar, in First Corinthians."

Dave read what was thrust under his nose. After a few moments, he started shaking his head again. "No, you can't just put two verses together like that."

"No, I'm not doing that. There's other passages too ... Mark's Gospel, for instance. '*At that time, men will see the Son of Man coming in clouds with great power and glory; and he will send his angels and gather his chosen from the four winds, from the ends of the earth ...*'. Just like in St. Luke and St. Paul. It's all *this* that we're missing."

"No ... you can't just dismiss what we've been taught like that. Nearly everyone says that the Rapture of the saints happens before the Great Distress, the Tribulation ..."

Bob punched a fist into an open palm. "That's another thing. Time and again, I'm seeing that God limits the time of the Great Distress for the sake of the saints. It doesn't say that He takes them off before it happens – they go through it, and He shortens it for their sake. And all through The Revelation, I'm seeing; '*Here is a call for the patient endurance of the saints*' – which says to me, they are going through it all."

"Well, OK then, that's more or less the mid-Tribulation view; the Rapture takes place a short way into the Great Distress."

"But that's not what I'm reading here. Even with your mid-Tribulation theory, we should still be already seeing the Great Distress – we should be in the middle of it. And I still say that we should expect all the world to see the Son of Man coming, just before or at exactly the same time as the Gathering of the Saints."

"Bob – you're doing my head in. I didn't come for a theology debate ..."

"Sorry, Dave." Bob held his hands up. "I'm sorry, mate. Maybe I *am* clutching at straws or something. But my gut tells me, *this is not what we think it is*." He stopped pacing and sat down opposite Dave. "And d'you know something else my gut tells me? You would be one of the *last* people to get left behind. You and Marie, both."

Dave managed a bleak smile. "Thanks, Bob." He took another swig of sherry. "And I'd say the same about you, too."

Bob smiled slightly, and then sighed. "So what *is* it that's happened? I don't know. It doesn't fit our usual theology. But I'm going to find out ... Is Marie frightened?"

"I left her in tears."

"Then I owe it to you and Marie. I'm going to find out."

"How?"

"Study and prayer, old pal."

Dave was looking drawn again.

"But if we really have been, you know, left behind – will He hear us?"

"The Lord hears *all* who call upon Him, my friend – all who call upon Him in truth. So it's going to be prayer. And getting on with my responsibilities – I've got a stack of accounts to sort for the taxman."

"Render to Caesar?"

"Yep. And after that – well, I'll keep you posted."

"God bless you, Bob. You are such an encouragement."

"You too. On both counts."

—

If Dave had still owned a car, and had driven to Bob's and back, he would have missed it altogether. But he was cycling, and cut through the pedestrian precinct.

The Baptists were among the few congregations who had retained their own building, because all their national leaders had signed up to the Proselytising Convention. In theory, no Baptist would speak of his or her faith to anyone except to answer a direct question; although a bold few still found ways around that.

There was something different about the building; Dave noticed it in the way that you do when someone has cut a tree down – you know at once that what you are seeing doesn't tie up with memory, but it takes you several moments to see *what* has changed.

There was not normally a man on the top window-ledge.

Dave skidded to a halt and looked up appalled. It was Jim Stone.

People were just beginning to gather, but there were no police or anything yet.

Dave threw his bike down on the paved front yard and sprinted up the steps. He threw himself at the front door and nearly knocked all the breath out of his body – it was locked. The side gate was ajar.

He staggered down the steps and ran up the side alley. The vestry door opened when he put his shoulder to it. Where were the stairs? There were two sets, he thought – he needed the front ones, up to the balcony, and up again. He ran gasping through the dilapidated rows of hard chairs in the silent, musty auditorium. There was an ache in his ribs, but he dare not slow down. *Jim, don't jump.* He clattered up the stairs to the balcony, and cast around for the second flight. There, in the corner – a spiral staircase. He was slowing down now, despite himself. *Oh, Jim, don't jump, don't.* He came wheezing out at the top into an old Sunday school room, thick with dust. The window was open.

"Jim! It's me, Dave. Hold on! Don't ... don't do anything. Where are you?"

He put his head out of the window, made the mistake of looking down, nearly fainted, grabbed the sill with both hands.

Jim was on the ledge, only a metre and a half away. Too far to grab.

"Jim, mate! It's Dave. Dave from the house ch – you know," he hastily corrected himself.

There was a crowd gathering below by now. Glancing at them made him shut his eyes for a moment and tighten his white-knuckle grip on the window frame. "Talk to me, Jim. What is it?"

Jim was standing on the pollution-eaten cornice, heels to the wall, his toes at the very edge. The wind was snatching at his hair, blowing it off his bald spot and into his eyes. He didn't seem to notice. Nor did he say anything.

"Jim, mate. Talk to me. You can tell me what's the matter. I'm your friend, Dave. Please, mate, talk to me." He was trying desperately not to say '*don't jump*'; weren't you supposed to keep the suicide's mind off it?

"Don't come out here, Dave," said Jim finally. "No need for you to get involved."

"Jim! You're my friend. Of course I'm involved." Jim shook his head, and looked at him for the first time. "You don't understand ..."

"Then tell me, Jim. What don't I understand? Please, explain it to me. At least."

"I've led them astray, Dave. Led them all astray. My deacons were right, and I was wrong. All those years, and now all those lives. My fault, Dave. I can't stay here ..."

He turned back, and appeared to bracing himself to step forward.

"Jim! Stop! This won't solve anything. Please!" Dave's voice was cracking with desperation. "You haven't explained yet! *What's* your fault? Tell me!"

Jim stopped. He turned his head again. Something strange was flickering in his face; it was some moments before Dave realised it was flashing blue lights from below.

"I've led them all astray," he said again. "I taught them all the wrong things. George and Edward – my deacons – they told me. If only I'd listened. I taught the people the old-fashioned virtues – love, and devotion, prayer, worship; forgiving one another, helping the disadvantaged ... Philip told me, too – the world's moved on, our faith must move with the times – he always said that ..." His eyes were moist. "And now they're taken up, and all my people are left behind. That's what I've done. *That's* my fault."

Left behind. That awful, bone-chilling phrase again. What could you say to it?

"Jim, listen a minute. How was it wrong to teach people to love one another? To pray, to worship, to read their Bibles, to stick close to God? To forgive? To help each other, and the poor and needy? You weren't wrong, mate. How could that be wrong?"

"But it *was* wrong. I've failed them in the worst way possible. I've condemned their souls to a Christless eternity. Don't you see it?" Suddenly Jim was looking him straight in the eye. "Don't you *realise* what's happened here? This was the Ingathering, the Rapture of the Saints. Do you not see that?"

Dave swallowed hard. "Yes, Jim; I know what it looks like."

"Looks like?" Jim could almost have been back in his pulpit for a few moments. "It's the end of all things that is upon us. It's in that song, when you and I were children;

There's no time to change your mind,
The Son has come
And you've been left behind ..."

"But, Jim, this won't ... This won't get anyone into heaven. Just stay and listen to me for a minute. Please."

"I know this won't get anyone into heaven. Least of all me! But I don't deserve heaven! This is the only way I can apologise to them. For getting them left behind."

"Jim, wait. Listen." He took a deep breath. "I'm not so sure anymore. It might *not* be the Gathering. There's too much that doesn't fit."

What was he doing? Agreeing with Bob? Just talking down a jumper?

"Not the ... But what else could it be? No, no, it's the only thing it *can* be!"

"I've been talking with Bob – he's been looking at the Scriptures again ..."

At that moment a firm hand on his shoulder almost made him jump out of his skin. A police officer and two firemen were behind him, another two were tiptoeing off with a heavy shapeless bundle and a tripod to somewhere the other side of Jim. More uniforms were quietly filling the room.

"Just move aside, will you, sir," said the officer, firmly starting to draw him back from the window.

"Look, officer, I'm a friend, and I –"

"Just leave this to us, sir," replied the officer in a tone that offered no room for negotiation. He continued to manoeuvre Dave away from the window-sill.

"Bob's still here?" Jim was asking as Dave was pulled out of sight. His last impression of Jim was of a face transfixed in amazement.

"Yes, Bob's still here!" called Dave. "And I'll tell you something else —"

They did it with alarming speed and efficiency; the bundle was flung out of the far window, by the thing on the tripod, straight across Jim to the firemen waiting at the near window. They caught the end of it as it turned into a net, and secured it in a flash behind the windows, pinning Jim to the wall.

"– There's no way *you'd* have got left behind, Jim! No way at all!"

"That's quite enough of *that,* sir, thank you," said the officer, bundling Dave towards the stairs. Another officer was at the window, apparently addressing Jim. "Now then sir, you're under arrest for attempted self-harm and causing a breach of the peace. Name?"

———

Marie looked up as he came in. She didn't seem to have moved from her seat.

"You were a long while with Bob, darling."

"I wasn't just with Bob," Dave groaned as he slumped into the sofa. "I was talking Jim down off a ledge."

"What!?"

"Jim was going to – well, end it all. He said he'd let all his people down, taught them wrong, and got them ... left behind." He was still finding those words difficult.

"Is he ...?"

"He didn't jump. The police arrested him."

"Oh, no."

"For attempted suicide."

"Will they let him out?"

Dave had been mulling that one over on the way home.

"We'll just have to pray that they don't 'section' him for religious fervour."

"Oh — poor Jim. Oh Dave, it's just too awful, too awful." Her shoulders began to shake again, and he pulled her in and held her tight, his own eyes moistening.

Moments later the doorbell rang.

Dave answered it.

"Naomi! Poppet, how are you?" He swept his

nine-year-old daughter up into his arms. "I'd forgotten you'd be home for the holidays today."

"Sign here, please," said the lady with the clipboard. He managed to oblige without having to put his daughter down. She was hanging on with legs as well as arms.

"Ten o'clock a week next Tuesday, then," said the lady curtly. "Don't be late." She clicked primly back to the minibus.

"It's so good to see you again, sweetheart," sighed Dave. He left her luggage on the step for the moment, and carried her inside in a bear-hug to deposit her on Marie's lap.

"You've been crying," Naomi was saying to her mother as he came back in with the luggage. "And so have you, Dad," she added reproachfully.

"Oh ... it's nothing," Marie began to say, and then contradicted herself by bursting into tears again. Dave took a few minutes attempting to explain, in as low-key a way as he could.

There was no fooling Naomi.

"So you guys think Jesus has come, and left you behind?"

"That's what it looks like, yes."

"So how come no-one else saw Him? Why didn't

I see Him?"

There was really no good answer. "We don't know, love."

She thought for a moment. "So who did He take?"

"Well ... no-one's seen Uncle George; or Isobel; or Maurice Brown, or Diana who comes to the prayer meetings here ... or Mr Whitworth ... or Mr. Turnbull ..."

She looked disgusted. "Why would Jesus want to take *them?*"

Dave and Marie exchanged glances. "Whatever do you mean, sweetheart?"

She was on her way to the fridge, opening the door and scowling inside at the contents.

"Can I have some juice?"

"Of course, darling, help yourself. — What do you mean, exactly?"

"Well, if *I* were Jesus, I wouldn't choose them," she called through from the kitchen. She came back through with a big glass of orange juice. "I'd have Uncle Bob, for one – is he still here?"

"Yes."

"He always makes me think of Jesus. And I'd have Mr Stone from the Baptists, he's scrummy.

And Alison, and – oh, lots of other people; but I wouldn't have any of *them*."

They hardly dared ask. Dave cleared his throat. "Why's that, sweetheart?"

"Well, Uncle George is very nice to me, but he's nasty about other people. He stopped Mr. Stone from getting that nice lady in to organise our youth thing, and now it's not going to happen. Him and Mr. Whitworth stopped it." This was the neighbourhood-help project planned for the summer. Kids in all the churches had been looking forward to it, but it had folded when the Baptists pulled out, and Dave and Marie hadn't known why until this moment.

"And Isobel is horrid. She bullies you into taking those envelopes round to people who don't want them, and it's like it's your fault when you bring them back empty."

Marie was biting her lip. "Oh, darling, she's only wanting to help poor people ..."

"She isn't really. *I* don't think she is. She wants everybody to say how well she does. We have to do it for her, and she gets all the pats on the back."

Dave was about to say something, but didn't.

"And maybe Jesus felt he had to take Pastor Turnbull 'cos he's a pastor. But he's so up himself —"

"Naomi!"

"Well, he is."

"Maybe, but we shouldn't say it."

"Somebody ought to say it. And who else? Mr. Brown?"

"Yes ..."

"He's not nice. He slaps Alison around."

Dave and Marie were both on the edges of their seats. "How do you know that?"

"When I've stayed overnight with Kirsty." Maurice and Alison's daughter was one of her best friends. "I've heard them, downstairs. He does all the shouting. Kirsty cries in her pillow when he does it."

"But — you don't actually know he *hits* Alison, surely?"

"Oh yes. Not just 'cos Kirsty told me. One morning she had all one side of her face red. I saw it. She didn't want me to notice."

Marie decided to change the subject. "What about us, darling? Would you choose us?"

"Of course I'd choose you, Mum. And Dad. You'd be the *first.* Didn't I say?"

———

Finally, something about it made the news that night.

It was only the regional news, and it was the throwaway story at the end; a traditional Easter Saturday ordination had to be postponed because no-one could find the bishop. To make it more intriguing, no-one could find nine of the twelve ordinands either, nor the archdeacon; so someone had to stand up in a cathedral full of mixed-faith attendees and apologise for "a delay due to unforeseen apocalypses", which was of course a slip of the tongue, but gave the reporters some fun.

"You haven't eaten all day, have you?" remarked Marie. "Let me get you some tea."

"No ... I'm not sure that I want any. Bob's doing some Bible study on this whole situation – I promised I'd pray, and I think I'll fast too. D'you mind?"

She smiled. It was like a brief ray of sun. "Of course not. I'll join you."

Later that evening, the phone rang. It was Bob.

"Dave, how's Marie?"

"A bit better now, thanks. I'm glad you called; remind me in a minute, I've got something funny to tell you."

"And I you, old man. You know I've been doing the tax accounts today?"

"Right."

"Well, I've been looking at how much people have been giving. Now – I'm mentioning no names, OK, but I've noticed a very strange thing ..."

"Go on."

"The people who – er – we can't contact, yes?" Bob was apparently being careful for eavesdroppers, which was not unknown. "I now make it eleven of ours, by the way."

"Eleven?"

"Yes. Here's the thing. Not one of them, by my reckoning, is giving a noticeable percentage of their income. And nearly all of the remainder are giving proportionately more than the best of the eleven."

Dave digested that for a moment.

"Couldn't they be putting money in without pledging it?"

"No, I'm not just counting Gift Aid pledges. Everything is now in envelopes – you're obliged to register all your giving now, taxed or not, pledged or not, remember?"

"Of course."

"Now I know what you're going to say next."

"We're not under the law of Moses, we're under grace?"

"Exactly. There's no law, these days, that says that we must give ten percent."

"Right. What's the 'but'?"

"But – in the past I've found it a pretty good indicator – a litmus paper – for commitment in other areas. If you're not prepared to put your money into something, are you really putting your heart in? Are you with me?"

"Like the saying, 'Put your money where your mouth is'?"

"Or like, 'Where your treasure is, there will your heart be'."

"I think I get your drift."

"Thing is, Dave, I know I could be up a gum tree, and completely wrong; but the more I look at this ... thing, the more puzzled I am by *who's* gone off the radar. It looks less and less like the people you'd expect."

"Well, you know I was arguing with you earlier, but on that point I'm beginning to agree. It's not stacking up. Did you hear about Jim Stone?"

Bob hadn't, so Dave told him.

"That's awful ... and all because he thought it was his fault. *Jim,* I ask you."

"Yes, but we can't see it ourselves, can we? I mean, you and I can look at Jim and say 'Now there's a true, humble man of God', but he can't see it himself."

"He'd be the less humble if he did."

"You could be right. Do you know, I think he was knocked sideways to hear that *you* were still around. It was about the last thing I could tell him before they arrested him. That, and the fact that *he* would be one I'd never leave behind, if I were Jesus."

Bob sighed. "I'll be praying for him … You said you had something funny to say."

"Well, Bob, the funny thing I had to tell you is very similar to yours, but from another angle."

"Really? No kidding."

"Naomi's home today. She sussed something was

up, and in the end we told her. Guess what her reaction was."

"You tell me."

"She said, 'Why ever would He choose *them*?'"

"No!" There was a hint of a laugh in Bob's voice, for the first time in twenty-four hours.

"Straight up. Totally unprompted. And – this was scary – she had reasons to back it up for everyone we mentioned."

"No kidding?"

"Talk about taking no prisoners. You know what kids are like. She said – 'scuse me – that Pastor Turnbull was up himself —"

There was a guffaw at the other end.

"— And she reckoned Jesus must have been obliged to take him as he was a pastor."

"Priceless!"

"More seriously though, Bob – did you know that M – the guy who didn't turn up at the meeting, I mean – beats his wife?"

An immediate silence. Then: "No, I didn't."

"From what she's told me, there's precious little doubt. She's stayed at their house a few times, that's how she knows."

Another short silence.

"Kids are amazing, aren't they?"

"My one keeps me on my toes, I know."

"The stuff they come out with; no false shame ... they just tell it like it is."

"D'you know, Bob? I think it's just that they haven't had to pussyfoot around the truth all their lives. They don't have time for political correctness and skin-saving."

"You could well be right," sighed Bob.

"Us – we've been browbeaten, bargained into the ground. Don't say this, you might lose your job. Don't say that, they might take away your kids ..."

"Point taken, old pal."

"Oh, Bob – sorry, I'm ranting."

"No, you're quite right. We're all tarred with the same brush."

"Please, mate – I wasn't getting at you, really."

"No, Dave, I know you weren't," said Bob mildly. "But keep saying it; we all need to hear it ... Anyway, I've finished the accounts, I'm going to do some more study. See if I can come up with any answers. See you tomorrow at ten?"

"Tomorrow at ten it is. All the best, mate. Goodnight."

In bed, Marie lay awake, unable to sleep.

"Dave, love ..."

"Uh – huh."

"I've been thinking about the Great Distress."

Dave rolled over. "What about it, darling?"

"Could we be in it already?"

He blinked. "I wouldn't have thought so, my love ... what makes you ask?"

"I've been thinking – it's not so bad for us, really; but what about other places? So much of Africa, and all the Middle East and most of Asia – believers are getting thrown out of their jobs, and their homes are getting burned down ... thousands and thousands have been killed ... I'm sure we don't know the quarter of it. In America, you can't keep your kids at home and teach them if you're a believer, you can't set up a business, all sorts of things. In South America, they've had no end of trouble, riots and looting, all against the evangelicals, with no provocation. They've passed some new laws in Australia, it'll be worse than America soon."

"Well, I suppose ... it's not very much better here, if you want to look at it that way. We can't teach our own kids, or even have them at home except

81

for holidays. We can't have buildings, unless we agree never to proselytize, and all the other things. Any time we have a meeting, we have to notify the Board of Religious Affairs, in case they want to observe; you can be put in jail for speaking the name of Jesus in the wrong place, you can be put in a mental asylum for being too religious. And we take it all, and we survive somehow."

"But isn't it wrong? Isn't all this, persecution? Don't they say that you can get used to almost anything? That an abused child doesn't think of it as abuse, it's just life?"

"I don't know, love. But, at the moment, it's just that – it's just life …. Try and get some sleep." But then he was restless, remembering the verse: "*These are just the beginnings of the birth-pangs.*"

—

Easter Sunday was still officially a holiday, which meant one Sunday in the year when you could rely on being able to get together.

The congregation met outside a supermarket, in a quadrangle of shops which were all shut for the morning and where they would not disturb anyone. They had one guitar, one violin and a clarinet to assist with the songs.

"*Jesus Christ is risen today, Ha-a-a-le-lu-u-iah; Our triumphant holy day ...*"

Dave shut his eyes for a moment, remembering the Salvation Army band, not so many years ago, playing the same hymn on the same day in the same town centre, just two hundred yards from here, but right in amongst all the people, without shame or fear.

He opened his eyes and looked around at the congregation. It was even smaller today – you noticed the loss of eleven people overnight.

How many other people had spent a sleepless night, fretting over the probability that all they had believed, and worked for, over the years, had been in vain?

Faces were solemn, you couldn't deny it; many had deep pockets of grey under the eyes, there was no missing that. But all were singing bravely. Suddenly, Dave knew, as he looked at these faces, that these – the ones who were left – they were the ones whom he loved. *These* were the ones who would, if called upon, lay down their lives for him – and he for them.

The others had been the passengers. Even the prayer-group regulars – attendance was not the measure, it was some quality of the spirit, some inner commitment.

It was a typical Easter day, bright but chilly, with fat clouds chasing across the sky and every now and again threatening a shower. The service was not over-long.

When Neil, the worship leader (Neil! – what a heart for Jesus! Why in the world would he be left behind?) stopped, and asked if anyone had a Scripture, a word from God or a teaching, Bob stepped forward into the horseshoe.

"I believe I've got something very significant from the Lord for us all," he began.

"You'll be aware that some folk are missing today – folk who would normally never fail to be here. Some of us have loved ones who ... seem to have gone missing in the last forty-eight hours, and we are concerned. I've certainly been concerned."

He paused, and paced for a moment.

"I think most of us have concluded, very reasonably, that what we have seen over the last two days appears to be one of the events of the End of the Ages. And it's not good news for us

who are left; for this event, as we have been
taught, is called the Ingathering, the Rapture of
the Saints. It means – if we're right – that Christ
has gathered up those he counts as saints, and
that's not good news for those of us left behind."
Well, he's pulling no punches, thought Dave.
Good for you, Bob.

There was a stifled sob from somewhere at the
back. Dave thought it was Alison.

"Now I'm not a theologian, and I'm not a great
Bible scholar. I'm just an ordinary bloke who's
trying to make sense of it all. So you may or may
not accept what I'm about to say. That's fine – the
Scripture says to test any prophecy. So I'm asking
you to check it out before you accept it. I want to
say here and now that I could be up a gumtree,
and if I am, don't join me. Alright?"

The wind blew his hair over his eyes, just as it had
done to Jim. But Bob's face was a total contrast;
where Jim's had been hollow with despair, Bob's
was aglow with hope.

He's onto something, thought Dave. *It's the old
Bob again*.

"I was troubled by ... many of the details of this
event we've been seeing," Bob continued. "I was

troubled by a lot of things that didn't fit what I read in the Scripture – things we are told to expect, that I haven't seen; things I'm told won't happen, that have happened. For a start, those who've been left behind. Who knows Jim Stone?" Nods all across the audience.

"Who would agree that if we've got a man of God in our town, it's Jim?"

A murmur of agreement.

"I'm not going to go through it all," continued Bob, "but the more I looked, the less I understood why the Lord would pick out the ones who are gone, but leave the ones who are standing here – and in other congregations all over town. Young Neil here, now." Neil blushed down to his collar.

"When Neil picks up that guitar, I hear angels picking up theirs. When he begins to lead us in worship, I'm jet-propelled into the throne-room of God! Aren't you?" He turned to Neil, and gave him a bear-hug. "Who'd leave this saint behind?" he asked over Neil's shoulder.

He's sticking off the ones who've gone, thought Dave. *Probably a good move.*

"I know that you know the verses about the Lord's Second Coming," Bob continued. "I've been looking at them hard and long myself, because I know that if I can find an answer, I'll find it in the Scripture. Well, this is what I found, and it astounded me."

He paused, folded his hands together and put them to his mouth for a moment.

"First, I found that time and again, the Ingathering of the Saints is spoken of in the very same breath as the visible coming of the Son of Man – the sign seen by the whole world. Would you agree?" Nods all round. "And if anything, it happens not *before* this visible coming, but at the *same time*, or immediately *after*. Have you noticed this?" More nods, though fewer. "And has this sign appeared in the sky, over all the earth? Has it even made the ten o'clock news? If it did, I missed it." Most of Bob's audience were now lost in rapt attention.

"But the question is, If this event is *not* the Rapture of the Saints, what can it be?" Bob paused, and started to pace again. "This had me foxed all of yesterday. I read those passages over and over, I read Revelation, I read Daniel ... you know, the works."

He stopped. "But then I read around the proof texts, into the context a bit more. And I found *more* things that troubled me. When Jesus talks about 'One will be taken and another left', the disciples ask him 'Where, Lord?'"

He paused for a moment. "What does that mean? Well, what struck me – and OK, I may be wrong, but what struck me was – they are asking, '*Taken* where?' And what does Jesus reply? 'Where the corpse is, there will the vultures gather.'"

"Now that gave me a problem. What a weird thing to say if you're talking about the joyful gathering-up of the saints! Eh? It doesn't compute."

"But I looked further. And I found a passage in St Matthew that speaks of *another gathering*. One that suddenly makes much more sense. One that happens just *before* the End of the Ages." He paused. "Will you read it with me? It's the Parable of the Weeds."

He gave the chapter and verse, and there was a rustling of half a dozen pocket Bibles. People crowded round to share.

"I ought to say, before I read this," interjected Bob, "that this may offend some. I honestly mean no hurt to anyone stood here. Nor to anyone they've lost. Please bear with me, and I'll try to explain what God said in my heart as I read this."

The kingdom of heaven is like a landowner who sowed good seed in his field. But while everyone was sleeping, his enemy came and sowed weeds among the wheat, and went away. When the wheat sprouted and formed heads, the weeds also appeared. The owner's servants came to him and said, 'Sir, didn't you sow good seed in your field? Where then did the weeds come from?'

'An enemy has done this,' he replied.

The servants asked him, 'Do you want us to go and pull them up?'

'No,' he answered, 'because while you are pulling the weeds, you may root up the wheat with them. Let them grow together until harvest. At that time I will tell the harvesters; "First collect the weeds and tie them in bundles to be burned; then gather the wheat and bring it into my barn."'

"The disciples ask Jesus to explain the parable. He lays it all out very simply."

The one who sowed the good seed is the Son of Man. The field is the world, and the good seed stands for the sons of the kingdom. The weeds are the sons of the evil one, and the enemy who sows

them is the devil. The harvest is the end of the
age, and the harvesters are angels.

"I only want to pick out one more thing for you,
and it's in verse forty-one:

— so will it be at the end of the age. The Son of
Man will send out his angels, and they will weed
out of his kingdom everything that causes offence
and all who do wrong ...

"Now, please don't stop listening if you've just
lost someone you've loved, or someone you
respected. I'm sorry to offend; but just hear me
out, I'm almost done.

"What if what we have just seen is this gathering
described here? Think, not of who has gone, but
who's left. You're left. I look in your eyes and I
see lovers of God; I don't see sons of the devil.
Neil here is left, Dave and Marie – over the back
there – they're left, Jim Stone is left, dear old
saints – and young saints – I know, in every
church, are left. What are we left for, if I'm even
half right? Verse forty-three;"

Then the righteous shall shine like the sun in the
kingdom of their Father.

"This is our moment. This is our time to shine,
like never before. What does the Scripture say?

Hold up your heads, for your redemption is drawing near."

Bob was afire. His face seemed to be brighter than anything around him.

"And just consider for a moment – if our missing ones have been gathered ... in this way, then we must suppose they now stand before the judgment seat of Christ, to account for their lives. Did they really cause offence? It sounds very harsh. But could it be true? And if so, for what – some compromises? Some wrong attitudes? Some small but persistent sins?" His voice had dropped. "Just consider – *what sort of lives must we now lead,* if we are to remain as saints, shining in the kingdom of our Father?"

—

Lunch was postponed for half an hour. Marie and Naomi were on the Internet.

"We have to get this out, Bob," Dave was saying.

"Hope you don't mind waiting lunch."

"Not at all."

"You've given us hope. That's what we've all come away with."

"Well, thank God, not me – I was just the messenger boy. Just hope I got it right."

"I think you did. Just look at SAS – how we all came away today."

"How exactly?"

"Let's just say – shaken *and* stirred."

Bob smiled. "Well, again, if it was any good, it was God."

"God still needs willing messengers, mate. And there's got to be so many out there – thousands, could be millions – who need hope. Pastors standing on ledges, like Jim."

"Let's hope we can catch them in time."

"Thank God we've still got one channel."

The word of hope streamed silently out through countless computer nodes, spreading in minutes via bulletin boards and mail lists, flooding the world.

Reach Unto Heaven

It was a project that had been dreamed about for years – probably from the turn of the millennium; a new way of conquering that first great hurdle into space, Earth's gravity.

The theory was, that if you could suspend a long enough rope out beyond the atmosphere, it might eventually become self-supporting, due to the centrifugal force from the earth's rotation. Then, instead of using vast amounts of fuel and energy to propel a tiny payload into orbit, you used a much smaller amount of energy to make the same load climb the cable. It was the Indian rope trick, on a massive scale.

What had made it reality was materials science, of course, and the technology to turn a laboratory discovery into a viable semi-continuous process. From the discovery of how to "grow" what was, in effect, a diamond in the form of a microscopic filament – the carbon nanotube – patient trial and error had finally come up with a process that could produce such a filament in long enough continuous pieces to spin into a visible strand, then a thread, then a cord, and finally a cable, light enough to be lifted to the edge of the Earth's atmosphere by high-altitude balloon, flexible and strong enough to withstand the stresses of its own weight, wind and weather ... at least, in theory.

Now the theory was to be put to the test.

Of course, everybody wanted to be part of the project – and by that, I mean every nation on earth. Here was the possibility of a way to share in the endless possibilities of Space, for a fraction of the cost and the expertise that had been needed until now. NASA and the European Space Agency bowed to international pressure and created a partnership with Russia, China, and India, and then opened it to all. With increased participation, the cost of the initial stake went down, and in the end ninety-seven countries had a share in the project in addition to the founders.

My part was, not surprisingly, small and relatively brief. It took an age for the diplomats and ministers to hammer out the terms and policies and overall agreements; almost as long for the multinational programmes and sub-programmes to be defined and agreed, and individual streams and projects to be proposed and fleshed out and competitively tendered. Eventually, like a wave from an undersea disturbance, fanning out and suddenly increasing in height as it hits shore, the project reached out to people like me and swept us up, thousands upon thousands of us, sucking us in with the thrill of history in the making.

Picture if you can the vast international project site, where construction was already gathering pace by the day, and the sheer excitement (and pride) of being part of it all. No-one had ever known a project like it in history, above all nothing with the direct involvement of such a number of nations.

I was managing the siting and commissioning of one of nearly a thousand annealing furnaces – just one tiny cog running a hundred smaller cogs in a machine of mind-boggling complexity. You could stand on the roof of the building in which I was working, and not actually see the edge of the site in any direction ... only the ring of mountains shimmering far away on the edge of the dusty plain. The centre of the site – from which all the rest fanned out – was clearly marked by twenty-odd huge Ferris wheels where the pencil-thick ropes would be turned from horizontal to vertical, to be laid into the final cable, no thicker than a child's wrist, that would ascend into the heavens.

It was about the end of the first month on site, in the bustle of the endless detail planning, juggling with dependencies, identifying and countering risks, and all the hundred and one things that go with starting up a project within a huge programme, when the first straws in the wind came.

Raj, my technical lead, walked into the planning office one day and said:
"Dave – did you know the Americans are still using imperial units on their furnaces?"
I stopped what I was doing, and replayed his words in my head. "Not metric units?"
"No – pounds per square inch, would you believe. And Fahrenheit degrees."
I scratched my head in disbelief. "I thought metric units were agreed at the outset."
"So did I. Seems the Yanks are just doing their own sweet thing, again."
"Well ..." I paused, then shrugged. "Just one more issue to be aware of, I suppose. Make sure

everyone knows – and put in a double-check on all the data they send us."

About a week later, Dinos, one of my team leads, stopped me in the corridor. "Dave, have you heard about the argument over the vacuum gauges?"
"No – what argument?"
"Well, there's been a mix-up. We've been sent the German ones, and they're calibrated in kilogrammes per square centimetre."
I thought for a moment. "Well, not our problem. Send them to the Germans."
"Yes, I phoned them and told them – but they're telling me that all of us are using the same gauges, or at least the same units of measure – and they've already got gauges."
"Wait a minute. Kilos per square centimetre aren't ISO units, surely?"
"No – we're supposed to use megapascals. And we don't even know if these are kilogrammes-*force* per square cm. or kilogrammes-*weight*. It's a tenfold difference."

Over the next few days we found that over half the other furnaces in our cluster were using non-standard units. The Americans were of course using pounds per square inch, only they were using pounds-weight, whereas the Canadians were using pounds-force; the Germans were using kilogrammes-force, but the Russians and Poles were using kilogrammes-weight per square centimetre; the Italians were using torr; the French and the Chinese were using bar; New Zealand were using percent of a standard atmosphere; and for reasons known only to themselves, the Indians, Pakistanis and South Africans were using millimetres of mercury.

The cluster, or sub-programme, meeting did not go well that week.

We found part of the issue was the agreement at top programme level, which had only specified "Metric" units, not "international standard metric" ones. This should have brought at least some of the dissenters into line, but only Canada wavered – the US just took the attitude that they had installed their own standard equipment, and it was too late to change, so – tough. In the end, Canada took the same stance. India insisted that measuring pressure with a mercury column was the oldest and original standard, and millimetres were metric; so in the end nothing changed, except we each decided to take on an extra administrator to perform and check technical conversions.

It seemed a slight over-reaction at the time, but it was soon justified; our furnace was calibrated to degrees Kelvin, or "absolute" temperature, whereas the Americans, Canadians and South Africans were using Fahrenheit, half of the Europeans were using plain Centigrade, and the French and Russians were using the Reamur scale – God knows why. And the more we dug, the more anomalies we found.

Raj told me a week or two later that he still had concerns, to do with the conversion ratios, expansion coefficients, and tolerances. He tried to explain it to me, but I couldn't understand it all; at times, it sounded as if he was lapsing into Hindi trying to express what he meant.
The root of the problem was that some of our machinery was indirectly linked, via the tension in the spun filaments; if that went out of balance by even a small amount, we would get a rapid increase in individual fibre breakages and the

resultant thread, cord and cable would be weakened by an unpredictable amount.

Almost every day after that we encountered a new problem; sometimes to do with interpretation of the common standards, sometimes more to do with national pride, and sometimes just plain miscommunication. I can't even recall half of them now. Looking back at the notes in my logbook, they get more and more terse and frantic by the day, and now I can't even interpret a lot of them myself. The delays became unacceptable, and all the planned contingency was rapidly disappearing.

Perhaps unwisely, we tried to keep a lid on it all, at least the scale and depth of the issues. I swore my team to silence, as I suspect most other project managers did. After all, few things are worse on the CV than being a PM on the sub-programme that held back, or seriously compromised, the biggest prestige international project in living memory.

It would have been desperately embarrassing, but probably not fatal to the enterprise, if our sub-programme had been the only one to encounter that level of problems and confusion; however, increasingly we heard whispers that similar problems were happening all over the site.

At last, when the lid was impossible to keep closed any longer, we had the big programme meeting – which has passed into project-manager folklore now.
I was there, with about five thousand other PMs and stream managers, near the back.

Apart from the fact that about ten very senior people – I'm not sure if they were programme directors or politicians – harangued us in turn, I can hardly remember anything of what we were told; so I can't tell you which of the dozen or so versions of events you may have heard is closest to what was really said, or in what order. One thing I can confirm, though, is that the meeting really did break up in confusion after about three hours; and another thing is that none of the project managers I spoke to afterwards had any clearer idea of what we were supposed to do about everything than I did. And that was, no idea at all.

There was one further event I should tell you about. I had booked a full team meeting for the morning of the following day, so that I could relay to them the outcome of the big meeting. I tried to jot down as much as I could remember, which was not much, and to pick out any clear overall decisions and orders, which was next to nothing. As I tried to present the little I had gleaned, I noticed a peculiar look growing on the faces of all my team, which I finally identified as increasing bewilderment.

I staggered through to the end of what I had to say and asked for questions.

Raj put his hand up, and I nodded to him.

As he rambled on, I realised that I wasn't properly understanding any of what he was saying. I stopped him and asked him to go over it again. Francesca interrupted, and tried to explain; but it wasn't any clearer from her either, nor from Dinos, who tried next.

By this time several people were starting to talk at once. "One at a time!" I shouted, but the opposite happened; everyone joined in, and in the hubbub, it seemed as if they were all lapsing into their own first languages, and forgetting that the rest of us needed to understand them.

I had the advantage of the microphone. "Will you all speak the language of the country, please!" I shouted.

There was dead silence.
It was at least a minute before I realised what I had said.

The team broke up that same day. We all sneaked away, packed up, and quietly left site. We all knew there was nothing more to be said, nothing more that could be done. Some of us met briefly at the railway station, others at the airport; we nodded to one another, smiled sheepishly, and went our separate ways.

And that was how it all ended.
I think every team, every sub-programme, broke up over the following forty-eight hours; by the third day, the news had broken, and TV crews and helicopters were sending back films of the vast, desolate, almost-finished site; the radiating clusters of idle plant and empty buildings, the huge high-altitude balloon canopies deflated and forlorn amidst the Ferris wheels.

What made me realise the situation was, of course, the last thing I'd said to my team; which

was not exactly as I wrote a moment ago. It was:
"Siaradwch Gymraeg, os gwelwch yn dda!"

Since I left the project, I have been re-learning
English – so that I could tell you the story, of why
we never achieved the dream;
"Come, let us build a city and a tower, whose top
may reach unto heaven ..."

Leap of Faith

I was mowing the lawn.

It needed it. The front garden was looking untidy.

I stopped to empty the grass box.

"Hello," said the little girl.

Two deep brown eyes twinkled seriously at me.

"Play hopscotch with me," she said.

I straightened up.

There was the hopscotch grid, chalked on the pavement just in front of my lawn.

"I'm mowing the lawn," I said. "I'm busy right now."

"Is it important?" she asked.

"Important?" I pondered. "Well, I need to make the garden look better."

"I bet it's not as important as hopscotch," she said.

"What's so important about hopscotch?"

She looked me straight in the eye.

"You can change the world," she said. "If you do it right."

I laughed.

"Seriously," she said. "But you have to finish the game."

"And how long does that take?"

"Oh, just a few minutes."

I turned to empty the grass box.

"Don't you want to change the world?" she asked. "It's easy."

I turned back again.

"I've never played hopscotch," I said.

"Never?"

"Don't think so."

"I'll teach you," she said. "It's really easy."

She smiled at me. She won.

"Well … just five minutes then. Is that enough?"

"Yes. You can finish the game in five minutes."

I stepped over the flower border onto the pavement.

"You stand here," she said, "and you throw the pebble. Try and get the last square."

I threw the pebble.

It bounced, twice, and stopped right in the middle of the last square.

The girl clapped her hands. "That's right! Now you have to jump."

"How do I jump, exactly?"

"I'll show you." She stood on the first square.

"You go: right, together, left, together, right, together, BOTH – like that. And then you pick the pebble up."

She smiled at me from the far end of the grid.

"Now you do it. – You *must* keep your eyes on the pebble."

"Is that the rule?"

"It is, if you want to change the world."

"Why?"

She put her hands on her hips.

"It's just the rule, that's why. Now are you going to play?"

"All right."

She smiled. "Good."

"Remind me; was it left foot first?"

"It's right, together, then left, together." Her eyes were full of encouragement.

I stood on the first square, fixed my eyes on the pebble, and jumped.

Right, together, left, together, right, together, BOTH.

I bent down and picked up the pebble.

Everything changed.

My peripheral vision said everything, except the pebble and the square, had changed.

The hair on my neck stood up. I stood up.

Nothing had changed.

What had changed?

It was still my street, my house, my lawn. My mower. The sun still shone.

It was still my over-the-road neighbour, whose name I didn't know, walking his dog.

"Hello," I said to him with a smile. I don't know why.

"Hello," he said, with a smile. He stopped.

"D'you know, I'm sorry, we've been neighbours a year or more, but I don't think I know your name." He held out his hand.

"I'm John," I said. I shook his hand.

"I'm Mike," he said. "You've got a lovely garden. Always admire it."

"It's a bit untidy," I said. "I don't mow the grass as often as I should. Or weed it."

"Oh, do any of us?" he said. "And your hedge, at the side. Love it."

"Really?" Hasn't he seen all the litter that gets in it? I wondered.

"Yes, and the rose growing up the tree and all."

Rose? I thought. It was only a briar. I'd left it to discourage the local kids from climbing up the tree and breaking it again.

I looked. Yellow roses were breaking bud, all the way up inside the tree.

The hedge was litter-free.

"Look, we must get to know you better. D'you want to drop in for coffee some time? We're in for the next three evenings, Jane and I. Just pop round, you and your wife."

"Well … that's very kind of you …"

"Not at all. I should have asked earlier. Seriously, any time – just come and knock. See you soon."

He left, with a cheery wave. His dog hadn't fouled my flowerbed.

"I told you," said the little girl.

I was hardly listening.

The local boys were all playing football on the green across the way. Someone had just scored a goal; there was a cheer, but no boos. There were shouts, but no quarrels. Everybody seemed to pat everyone else on the back, and the game resumed. Someone was up a ladder fixing a gutter. But it was the man from No.10, fixing it for the lady at No.8.

A motorcycle went past. It went quietly, and not too fast.

What was changed? Everything was changed.

"Hello John!" called a voice. It was Dave, my over-the-back neighbour this time.

"Oh, hello, Dave."

"Your garden's looking lovely, as usual. How's your back now?"

"My back? A lot better than it was, thanks." I didn't know he knew I'd hurt it.

"Good! Thank God. Few things worse than a bad back."

I'd never heard old Dave say such a thing. Thank God? And no moans?

"And how're you, Dave?"

"Oh, not bad. Can't complain. Anyway, got to go – look after yourself."

He left me open-mouthed.

I started to walk down the street. Everything was the same, but different.

People were chatting over gates, over fences.

A young lad in a red car came around the corner just as I was about to cross the road. He stopped, beckoned me to cross, smiled.

A toddler was running away from its mother. The mother called – once – firmly, but kindly. The child stopped, and waited for the mother.

It was the people that had changed.

I headed for the corner shop.

The sour-faced old crone who usually served – would she still be there?

Yes, she was.

Her face broke into a wonderful, many-crinkled smile as I entered.

I smiled back. I couldn't help it.

"Did you leave your change behind, my dear?" she asked.

"My change?"

"Yes – was it you who bought a book of stamps this morning?"

"No … I've not been in."

"Ah, then it must have been the other gentleman. Anyway, can I help you?"

———

"You didn't finish the game," said a voice by my elbow.

The little girl was looking up at me reproachfully.

"Didn't finish?"

"No. And you said you only had five minutes."

"So I did … What do I have to do?"

"You have to jump back."

I let her lead me to the hopscotch grid, chalked on the pavement.

We stood at the last square.

"How do I jump back?"

"It's the same as the way you came. Throw the pebble. Try and get the first square."

I threw the pebble. It bounced, twice, and stopped right in the first square.

"That's good! Now do you remember how to jump?"

"I go right, together, left, together, right, together, BOTH."

"Yes, and what else?"

"Keep my eyes on the pebble?"

"That's right. And it's very important."

I jumped. Right, together, left, together, right, together, *both*. I picked up the pebble.

The world went grey and cold.

Everything had changed, and everything was the same again.

The sun still shone.

There was broken glass in the hedge. The dog had fouled my flowers.

Somewhere a mother was screaming at a disobedient child.

My heart choked me.

I turned. The little girl was still there.

"You said I could change the world," I said accusingly.

"You can," she said. "You started already."

"How?"

"You jumped, and you changed yourself," she replied.

"Where did I jump to? What world was that?"

"Where do you think you jumped to?" she asked innocently.

"It was like a world without sin," I said. "Where people actually care for each other."

"Yes," she said. "That's almost right."

"Almost?" I asked. "Was it … a world where people had never …" I couldn't finish.

"No," she said. "It's this world. Once it's changed."

"How can it change?"

"Like you did."

"But … I'm the same. I didn't change."

"Yes, you did. Because you jumped, and you saw."

"Why did you show me?"

"To change the world, of course."

"But I can't change the world."

"But you want to now, don't you?"

She smiled, and skipped away.

Judging Angels

A fantasy

"Excuse me sir, this way please," said a voice at my side. I was still craning my head round, trying to take it all in, waves of relief running over me. It *was* all true.

I let myself be steered to a small table where a blonde lady, with a lovely smile and dressed in a uniform entirely made of feathers, awaited me. She handed me a handkerchief as I sat down, and I realised my cheeks were wet. "Sorry," I mumbled, dabbing my eyes.

"That's quite all right, sir, you've had a bit of a rough journey here. Do you want to talk about it now? – or leave that till later?"

I thought of the motorway, the fool who pulled out, the jack-knifing tanker, the wall of traffic in my mirror ... and shuddered deeply. "Not now."

"Well then, let's get you started." She seemed to have all my details. "We've arranged for somewhere nice for you to stay; and your new job will be in the English division of the Courts. You'll start in the morning."

I blinked. "New job?"

"Oh yes. If we get you started right away, it'll help you settle in."

"But I don't know anything about the courts ..."

She beamed at me again. "Oh, you're fully qualified – remember what St. Paul said. Part of the job description after the earthly life? Judging angels?"

———

At the Courts I was introduced to my mentor, another courteous and professional person in a feather uniform. He first provided me with a gown (of course, I hadn't brought so much as an overnight bag with me) and introduced me to my duties.

"You'll be Assistant Clerk of the Third Court of the division," he explained.

"Oh ..." said I.

"You seem a little disappointed," he commented.

"Well, maybe ... I was told I would be judging angels."

He fixed a fatherly eye on me. "Let's put this in perspective," he said. "You remember what else St. Paul said? For instance about building in your earthly life with gold, silver and fine stone? Or with wood, hay and stubble?"

118

"Er – yes, I think I do."

"Well now, just one example. How many people did you befriend and lead to Christ?"

I gulped. "Umm ... maybe a half share in one?"

"And what other works you did, lead you to expect a reward here?"

I looked at my feet. "Not very much, I suppose."

"Well, cheer up then. You did enough to start as an Assistant Court Clerk."

My heart did a rebound. "Start as …? You mean I could go further?"

"Oh yes. Good use of talents is always rewarded with higher responsibility. As in the parable. And in any case, we have a job rotation scheme. A good Clerk will soon get a shot at trying a minor case – and so on."

"So – Assistant Clerk ... What does that involve?" I asked.

"You'll be required to look up legal matters as they arise in a hearing, and pass these to the Chief Clerk, who advises the judge."

"How – where – do I do that? What sort of legal matters?"

"Anything from the charges on the docket, to valid and invalid defences. And you can find it all on this system." He pointed to something very like a 21st-century PC screen. "You're looking a little puzzled again."

"I guess ... I hadn't expected it to be so like home – I mean the world. Or so *technological*."

He put a wing on my shoulder, and patted me with the hand underneath it. "You're very new here. You're seeing paradigms; everything is presented to you in terms you can grasp. Gradually, you'll see the truths behind these parables, and begin to live in those more and more; in the end, you won't need the parables, the pictures, at all. But believe me, it would completely overwhelm you *now* to experience heaven without the paradigms. Now – ready for your first lesson?"

———

The data system was not hard to get to grips with; in fact, it was beautifully laid out, consistent, logical and intuitive – perfectly designed for purpose, really. You entered a case number, and there was the docket, and hyperlinks to all the details, previous case law, etcetera. Or enter a charge, and its code, its definition, similar offences, even sentences given were at your fingertips.

Another thing I quickly learned was that the Courts were not there purely to try and punish; in fact they worked in a surprisingly similar way to the South African Truth and Reconciliation Commission. Offenders who appeared genuinely penitent were given the chance to confess all, and accept a sentence which merely gave them the opportunity to demonstrate their reform – five year's community service, for instance, needing dedication but over in a flash compared to eternity.

I asked my mentor about this. "Remember these are all angels," he commented. "This is their chance to put things right. It's a bit different for humans, as you know."

As time (or what seemed like time) went by, I became more and more familiar with both the legal side of things – the clear, pure, stern Law ever balanced with Grace – and the workings of the Court, which were somewhat similar to a magistrate's court in England. One judge heard the case; prosecution and defendant were allowed to speak (and call witnesses) in turn; and the judge's ruling and sentence were final. I never heard one decision appealed, nor did I ever see on the face of the accused that look of horror and disbelief when an innocent man is sent down unjustly.

———

Then one day (so to speak) I arrived at Court to find it astir. My mentor greeted me with "Ah, here he is. Court Two for you today, my man; and your first case!"

"What ...?"

"Did you not see the roster? You're to judge a case this morning. Here, slip off that clerk's robe, and put on this gown and cloak. And the laurel wreath."

In less than two minutes I was hurrying through new corridors behind my mentor. "What's on the docket?" I asked breathlessly.

"Ah, no need to go through that now; your Clerk will provide all the information you need, and it's territory you'll already be familiar with."

They got me to Court on time; gave me a quick refresher on procedure from a Judge's viewpoint; and after a final tweak to my gown and wreath, I entered the Court.

The accused angel seemed to do a double-take as our eyes met. I had never seen him before, but he seemed to know me; I thought for one moment he was going to ask to be tried in another Court, but he shut his mouth again and blushed to the tips of his feathers. I sat, and nodded to the Clerk.

The charges were read out. My mentor had been right; it was familiar territory indeed.

This angel, if the charges were accurate, had been some poor man's personal tempter, when he should have been his guardian angel from birth.

The accused pleaded "Not guilty"; instantly triggering two responses in me.

Firstly, as you would expect, "Oh dear; my first case and it looks like a long one."

Secondly, which I did not expect at all, a shock: "Where have I heard that voice?"

———

As the case unfolded, the shock deepened. This was not merely some poor man's story, of temptation sometimes resisted, just as often succumbed to. Too much, far too much was not merely familiar, it was *memory*. The unkindnesses to a younger sister, the secret disobediences of childhood, the thoughtless acts followed by panic in terror of punishment, the despising of boring rules (and indeed church observances); everything was there, right up to irritation with traffic that blunted my alertness and made the split-second difference that cost my family its father.

Everything was me. This was *my* tempter. What defence could he make before me?

The angel stood and started to stammer through a prepared speech. Before he was three sentences in, I had heard enough; I was certain of my verdict. I held up a hand. "In brief, what is the nature of your defence? That these things were never done?"

"I – well, my lord – I wanted to call witnesses ..."

"For nine out of ten of these charges, you could have only one witness, and he is before you in Court. Do you wish him to testify?"

"Ah – my lord – no, not at this time ..."

"Or do you wish to say, These things were done by another? That none of these words whispered were mine? Again, there is one in this Court who knows the voice that said them, and can testify."

"Ah – no my lord – I ... I did no wrong, my lord!"

"Again, there is one in this court who can testify to the peril placed upon his soul by these words and deeds, and the hurt to others they inspired, and the guilt he bore ..."

"But, my lord – surely the witness cannot also be the judge?"

All eyes were upon me. I stood. "Let it be known to this Court," I said, "that the accused is recognised by me as the tempter and tormentor of my soul upon earth."

I faced him again. "Did you really think that, in this Court, you would not face your victim?"

The angel had covered his face with his wings. The Clerk plucked at my sleeve, and whispered into my ear. I nodded.

"In accordance with the principles of this Court, and the Grace of the Most High, the accused shall be given a chance to change or reaffirm his plea and defence, before verdict is given. I declare a recess of one hour."

———

It was a relief to breathe fresh air again, taking a walk on the streets of gold, busy with a friendly, unhurried crowd, eternally lit by the Glory; very much like an Italian evening, but with the golden light of an English summer's afternoon. I sat down at a pavement café and asked for a coffee.

"Certainly, sir – large espresso? Con panna?" asked the angel, who also looked Italian.

"Exactly what I wanted," I replied, "thank you." Then I caught his eye. "Another paradigm, isn't it?"

"Of course, sir." He was back in no time. "Enjoy your paradigm, sir."

"My lord looks troubled," remarked a voice at my shoulder. It was an angel at the next table; I gestured to invite her to join me. "You are a judge, I take it?"

"Only for the day," I replied. "Most of the time I'm just a clerk of the court."

"Oh, but that's an honour in itself," she replied. "Many people are just happy to be here. That street-sweeper for instance. Ex-military, as you'd guess from the tattoos; a petty gangster before that. Just knew enough from the chaplain and a good barracks mate to pray 'Jesus, forgive me' the night before his vehicle hit a land mine."

I looked at the street sweeper. He was whistling something – possibly an old army hymn – and happy as Larry, wielding his broom.

"So ... a hard case, is it?" asked the angel.

"Tell me ..." I began. "Do we judge ourselves,

when we judge angels?"

"Ah," she replied. "Your first case ... I think the answer is, 'yes and no'. You may have thought and said and done many bad things — but you confessed, and threw yourself on His mercy, and were forgiven. Can you, in turn, forgive?"

I thought on that. "I think I must ... it's a condition of my own forgiveness, in a way, isn't it? Even though it's after the fact?"

She nodded.

"Thank you," I said.

My coffee was delicious.

———

I re-entered the court. All stood.

"This court is again in session ... How does the accused plead?"

My tempter lifted his chin. "I do not plead," he declared. "This court has no right to try me, and certainly not to condemn me."

A sigh, not of relief, ran across the court.

I weighed my words. "This Court has every right to try you," I replied, "and you leave me no option but to proceed to verdict and sentence.

"I, your judge, confess that each and every one of the ill words and deeds, cited in these charges, I did commit. I have already confessed them, at very least in general, in prayer, and accepted Heaven's forgiveness. I can therefore testify without further guilt that these thoughts, words and deeds were all prompted by the accused.

"I accepted as a condition of my forgiveness, that I too must forgive those who trespass against me, if only they relent. I was willing, but you were not. Grace and mercy were in my right hand but you refused them. Guilty you are, and guilty without remorse you are judged by this Court." The Clerk, during my speech, had quietly placed a four-cornered black cap by my left hand. It had small tassels at each corner, red like flame. Slowly and deliberately I now put it on my head.

The Archaeologists

Daniel sat back on his heels and wiped his brow. The dig was progressing well; more and more of the layer they were interested in was being exposed, almost intact. A couple of deeper shafts had established that the only activity below that appeared to have been many centuries of farming.

"Time for a break, Michael?"

His colleague straightened up, turned and gave him a grin.

"All right."

They laid down trowels and brushes, and carefully got up off their knees. Michael groaned and sighed.

"I'll soon be too old for this game."

"Hey, man, you're only seventy. What else would you do, anyway?"

"Oh … make science programmes. Become a museum curator."

They both chuckled, and walked carefully down the marked walkway to the awning. The latest finds were sitting bagged on the folding table, next to the water bottles.

"Chair?"

"Nah - it's nice to stand up for a bit."

Both of them stretched their arms and shoulders as they stood in the shade. Little yellow flags on canes at the corners of the dig twitched in the faint breeze. Heat shimmered on the red dirt beyond, on the dusty green scrub, on the two tones of grey of the flat surface they had uncovered.

"How far does it extend, do you think?"

"How far? No telling. Could be a couple of kilometres each way. Could be more."

They contemplated it silently for a minute or two.

"What were they like, do you think?"

"The people?"

"Yeah."

"Much like us, I guess. Different way of life, sure, but the people - no different from you 'n' me."

They gazed out over the dig again. Daniel slowly shook his head.

"Wonder if we'll ever really know."

"Know what? Why they died out?"

"Yeah. Are we any nearer finding out?"

Michael took another mouthful of water and thought a while before replying.

"There's a lot of theories around. Every dig we do sheds a little more light on it, I guess."

"What's your feeling on it?"

"Might be that it was a whole combination of things. People say it was climate change — but these folk were finding ways of coping with that. Other people say it was they ran out of key materials; but they were very inventive … Somehow, the whole civilisation became unsustainable, and they didn't see it coming until too late. Like Rome."

"The Roman Empire?"

"Yeah. Every civilisation, it seems, has an Achilles heel. Some things they don't want to change, so they ignore the warning signs. The First World — as they were called — wanted to get richer and stay on top. They relied on the resources and labour of the Third World and the Developing World. But the Developing World kept developing, and wanted more of the First World lifestyle. Maybe it was just unsustainable … They ran out of cheap resources, cheap labour, undeveloped places to exploit."

"Is that what you think did it?"

"It was a big part of it, sure. But there were other sides to it as well."

"Like what?"

"Well, they kept running out of water. They were using more 'n' more, all the time, but storing less and less. All these concrete surfaces, they would have been gardens once. But when every household had to have two incomes, and the old folks were put into care, there was no-one left to do the gardening; so they just concreted over, and all the rainwater just ran straight off. So they kept having floods, and then droughts."

"That's crazy, man."

"And when you use mineral resources, there's always some waste products. Stuff you can't recycle, or compost, or whatever. We know they had a problem with that. There's a theory they just kind of drowned in their own rubbish."

Daniel looked at him sideways. "Seriously, man? I heard they were into all kinds of ways of tackling that - carbon tariffs, landfill charges, laws about toxic waste …"

"Yeah, they did. But it was always a bit too little, a bit too late. See, they didn't want to give up their cushy lifestyle; and the Developing World producers just played along, for decades. First World wanted bright, shiny new appliances, so they made 'em, and didn't bother to make things that would last; that way, the First World would always be back for more bright shiny new stuff, and kept the factories in business, making money. No-one bothered with repairing things when you could buy a new one cheap enough."

"So the broken stuff, and the waste, just piled up?"

"That's right. Some of the old stuff and the broken stuff went to Africa, and Africa got pretty good at fixing things. They tried to send us their toxic waste, too, but after a while we stopped all that. And we reported them when they dumped it in coastal waters, too."

Daniel nodded thoughtfully. "So, you reckon that's why we survived and they didn't?"

"I reckon so. And tell you something else — our home, Pacific City, is built on their waste."

"What!! How come?"

"They used lots and lots of plastic — mostly to package stuff in. Appliances, durables, food, even water. And a lot of the plastic bags and bottles got away into the sea. By the turn of twenty-first century, there was a new Sargasso Sea — not seaweed, but a mat of mixed plastics, floating at the centre of the currents in the Pacific. It just built up and built up; no-one wanted to take responsibility for clearing it. And that's what we used as the foundation for Pacific City."

"You gotta be kidding me."

"No, straight up. I've seen it myself. If you go down to the jetties on the south side, and dive under to look, it's like a tight honeycomb of little plastic bottles, all with the caps pointing down and filled with air. Under the houses, of course, there are more layers — usually plastic foam, that was used to pack delicate things in transit. It lasts for centuries under water, like the bottles."

Daniel cracked a wide smile, got to his feet and shook his head. "Crazy, man."

"You go swimming off the jetties some time and jus' see if I'm right."

"Might just do that, man."

"And you know something else? Our airship, that's made from their waste, too."

"Now you are kidding me."

"Nope. Why d'you think it's all patchwork, like your mammy's bedspread? That's 'cos it's made from twenty-first century plastic bags, thousands of 'em. Heat-stitched together, they keep the helium in pretty well. Just think of that when

134

we're riding home. Ah well, time we got started again."

Michael adjusted his hat, and the two archaeologists trudged back out into the sun.

Friendly Fire

Special sitting of members of the Senate Committee on Defense, September 21, 20xx
Bench: Senator Bill Roberts (Chairman), Senator Bob Chiswell, Senator Andrea Doughty

CHAIR: This enquiry into events of last July 30th is being undertaken by a sub-group of the Senate Committee on Defense, in response to the demands by Congress to re-evaluate policy around autonomous military intervention capabilities presently deployed in the field. If we are ready to proceed?

CLERK: All present, Senator.

CHAIR: Then I first call Major General Waldegrave to the stand.

[General Waldegrave is sworn in]

CHAIR: General Waldegrave, you were the commanding officer over the 2nd Autonomous Intervention Unit, 105th Division, on the dates in question, am I correct?

GEN.W: Yes sir; 2nd AIU was deployed on active duty on those dates in the northern sector of the province of —

CHAIR: No need for the geography, General; we will refer, if necessary, to the location of operations by its code name as used by the Pentagon, which I believe is Zone Yellow Three.

136

GEN.W: Yes sir, that is correct.

CHAIR: Would you give us a brief synopsis of the situation on the morning of July 30th leading to the deployment of one of the 2nd AIU's vehicles?

GEN.W: Certainly, sir. We had received intel that a Special Forces deep-insertion unit, operating in the village of … should I use the codename, sir?

CHAIR: Yes please, General.

GEN.W: —Operating in the village known to us as City Tango 6, had been blown, and the three —

S. DOUGHTY: Excuse me, General. Blown meaning …?

GEN.W: Revealed, unmasked, ma'am. Identified by the enemy.

CHAIR: Go on, General.

GEN.W: Well, sir, our intel that morning was that there had been an immediate firefight. Some of our Special Forces were shot, but latest indications were that three or maybe four had survived. 2nd AIU was asked if we could dispatch a vehicle immediately to see if we could effect an extraction.

S. DOUGHTY: Meaning, I take it, to rescue the survivors?

GEN.W: Yes, ma'am.

CHAIR: At which point you dispatched a vehicle to the area?

GEN.W: Yes, sir. I requested Colonel Li to dispatch any suitable vehicle he had ready, and there was an AH-71 tricopter fuelled, armed and ready, so that was what we sent.

S. CHISWELL: Mr. Chairman, may I cut in here? Before we go any further into the narrative, I have some questions about the control of this tricopter.

GEN.W: With respect then, sir, I suggest you ask Colonel Li; this is his area of expertise.

CHAIR: Then let us call Colonel Li.

[Colonel Li is sworn in]

S. CHISWELL: Colonel Li, I understand you were controlling this tricopter sent to extract our men?

COL.L: No, sir, that's not correct. The AH-71 tricopter is a fully autonomous vehicle.

S. CHISWELL: Meaning no-one was controlling it? Then how did it know what it was sent to do?

COL.L: The mission is programmed into the AH-71 at the time of dispatch, sir. Thereafter, its onboard software takes full control.

S. CHISWELL: But what if it encounters a situation it hasn't been programmed for? Or an ambiguous scenario?

COL.L: The software is pretty comprehensive, sir, so that's a rare eventuality. But if it does, the vehicle will hold position, relay back the sensor information causing the ambiguity, and request an operational decision.

S. CHISWELL: So it will, if necessary, request human intervention?

COL.L: Yes sir, but only in exceptional circumstances.

S. CHISWELL: Did such an exceptional circumstance arise on this mission? Did the tricopter in fact request an operational decision while in the field?

COL.L: Yes sir, it did.

S. CHISWELL: Who was monitoring the tricopter when this request came through?

COL.L: That was Captain Vermaut, sir; but I was in the Ops Room at the time — that's the command centre, sir — and I took, or confirmed, the operational decisions that were made.

CHAIR: I think at this point we should return to the sequence of events. General, will you take over, or are you happy for the Colonel to continue?

GEN.W: The Colonel was on the spot, sir, and is best placed to give you the detail of events as they unfolded.

CHAIR: Very well. Colonel, please describe to us the events as you witnessed them, up to the point where intervention was required.

COL.L: Yes Senator. The AH-71 flew directly to the last known position of the deep-insertion unit — using

GPS coordinates transmitted by their field radio —
and arrived at 15:30 hours local time. It reported
taking evasive action due to small-arms fire shortly
before arrival; it then commenced a pattern search of
the area. To assist the search, we linked it to an aerial
survey drone we already had operating in the area.

S. CHISWELL: So that was the first intervention?

COL.L: That was just a routine intervention, sir,
normal operating procedure in those circumstances.

S. CHISWELL: Very well, carry on, Colonel.

COL.L: Yes sir. At around 16:15 hours, the drone
relayed a sighting of a group of men a few k's from
the centre of the search zone. On closer inspection, we
determined we had four men in full combat gear,
apparently escorting three prisoners in local costume.

S. CHISWELL: Was the drone just reporting to you
what it recognised, or did you actually have eyes-on?

COL.L: Both, sir; the drone reported what it deduced
from pattern-recognition, and we could see the relayed
video that confirmed it. At that point we believed we
had located the survivors of the firefight, and directed
the AH-71 to their reported location. We also
informed their command centre that we had a vehicle
on the way to effect extraction.

S. CHISWELL: What happened then?

COL.L: The AH-71 reached the location at 16:35 hours and spotted the seven men. It confirmed four in battle gear, with standard issue arms, and three in local native garb, apparently bound and gagged. The vehicle landed and opened the side door, to enable access.

S. DOUGHTY: One moment, Colonel. This tricopter — was it capable of holding all seven men?

COL.L: Yes, ma'am, at a push. However, we were concerned about the range with that sort of load — whether we could get them all home. I should add we were getting reports of adverse weather coming in.

S. CHISWELL: So what did you decide, Colonel? Did you intervene at this point?

COL.L: Not exactly, sir; we were just in the process of loading a modification to the mission.

S. CHISWELL: Which was?

COL.L: We knew, sir, there was another unit on patrol in Zone Yellow Two, about one-third of the way back to base. We judged it best if we instructed the AH-71 to rendezvous with that patrol and offload the prisoners.

S. CHISWELL: So then the tricopter could return to base with the four men?

COL.L: That was our intention, sir.

S. CHISWELL: Your intention, you say? So that was not what happened?

COL.L: No, sir.

S. CHISWELL: Go on, Colonel.

COL.L: Well, sir, three things happened close together. First, we were advised that the AH-71 was detecting gunfire close by. No hits were recorded on the vehicle.

S. CHISWELL: What was your response to that?

COL.L: We didn't have to respond, sir; the AH-71 judged that it should stay holding position for the men to board, and we saw no reason at that time to countermand that.

S. CHISWELL: What happened next?

COL.L: Well, sir, about the same time, we received a message from the other command centre — the one for the deep-insertion unit — that they had had no reply from their unit in the field.

S. DOUGHTY: Didn't that concern you?

COL.L: Not at the time, ma'am; these things happen in live operational situations.

S. CHISWELL: You said three things happened at once?

COL.L: Yes sir; the third thing was, we registered only four men getting aboard. This was our first indication of a problem. However, we didn't have eyes on the situation at the time; we were reliant on the AH-71 for our intel.

S. CHISWELL: What did you do?

COL.L: Well, the AH-71 was holding position, waiting for the remaining three men. We couldn't leave it there indefinitely. We did have the drone still in the area; we requested another fly-by to get visual on the situation. This we received at 16:45 hours.

S. CHISWELL: What did that reveal?

COL.L: Well, sir … [pauses] … the video showed us the three prisoners sprawled on the ground a few yards from the AH-71. They were not moving. We concluded that they had been shot. The other four men had boarded and left them, so we concluded they were not merely wounded. In view of this we authorised the AH-71 to take off. That was the first intervention.

S. DOUGHTY: You authorised the tricopter to take off, leaving three prisoners either dead or wounded on the ground?

COL.L: We had little choice, ma'am. We had not been able to contact the unit we were extracting, and we had to rely on their judgment of the situation on the ground.

CHAIR: We understand that, Colonel. What happened next?

COL.L: Well, sir, Captain Vermaut asked if we should revert the mission statement to fly the four men directly home, or leave it as it was to rendezvous with the patrol, and report. That way we would get the earliest intel on what had happened.

S. CHISWELL: And it was your decision to let the tricopter rendezvous with the patrol?

GEN.W: If I may interject, Senator? Colonel Li reported the events as we knew them at that time to me, and I endorsed his recommendation that the AH-71 should rendezvous with the patrol. I felt we needed the earliest possible explanation of events. I also notified their command.

CHAIR: Thank you, General. Please carry on, Colonel.

COL.L: Yes sir. The AH-71 was given the GPS coordinates of the patrol, and rendezvoused with them at 19:15, just before sunset. We had already passed a message to them that we, and their own command, wanted an initial debriefing from the four men before bringing them back to base. It was what happened next that led to the attempted second intervention.

CHAIR: Go on, Colonel.

COL.L: Well, sir, the side hatch was already open when the AH-71 was landing, and just before touchdown the vehicle reported gunfire, extremely close by. The next notification we had was that the patrol on the ground was firing on the AH-71, and the vehicle was returning fire from its chain gun.

S. DOUGHTY: The patrol was firing on our own tricopter?

COL.L: Yes, ma'am, and the AH-71 was firing on them. The next moment we were notified of a serious hit, possibly an RPG, and the AH-71 landed heavily. The last notifications we had were that the four occupants left the craft, and that all systems were shutting down due to fire. We had no time to intervene or interrogate the onboard computers.

GEN.W: I'll just add that when that happens, Senators, the computer systems self-destruct, to avoid capture by an enemy.

CHAIR: So when did you find out what had happened?

GEN.W: That was the following day, Senator. There were no other forces close by, and it was too late to get another patrol into the area before dark. The crash area was secured around midnight, and by 06:00 hours on the 31st we had retrieved the flight recorder. This, together with the data stream we had recorded during the operation, gave us enough information to reconstruct events.

CHAIR: So, to the best of your knowledge, what had transpired?

GEN.W: Our conclusion was, sir, that both we and the AH-71 had been fooled into thinking our men — the survivors of the deep-insertion unit — had taken prisoners and were ready for extraction. In fact, it was they who had been taken prisoner, and the enemy had forced them to exchange clothing. It was our men in local costume, bound and gagged, who were shot and left for dead. It was four insurgents who boarded the AH-71. At the rendezvous with the patrol, the insurgents on board the AH-71 opened fire; that was the "extremely close" gunfire that was reported. The patrol guessed correctly what was happening and returned fire; the AH-71 then registered them as hostile and opened up on them with the chain gun.

S. DOUGHTY: Were there any survivors?

COL.L: There were no survivors on our side, ma'am, although the last man standing managed to down the AH-71 with a shoulder-launched RPG. As far as we know, the four insurgents managed to get away.

CHAIR: So, in summary then, General, where do you see the responsibility lies for this tragic fiasco?

GEN.W: Sir, that's very difficult to say. Operational decisions had to be made on the data available. The pattern-recognition software appeared to give us the correct information at all points, and what we saw with our own eyes — relayed from the drone — didn't give us cause for doubt. And you simply cannot program an autonomous machine for every possible eventuality. The AH-71 did everything we could have expected of it.

S. DOUGHTY: Including wiping out our own patrol? Eight men?

GEN.W: Yes, ma'am, I'm afraid so. In a live-fire situation, hesitation is fatal. And the AH-71 seek-and-destroy mode is singularly efficient.

CHAIR: Well, thank you for your evidence, gentlemen. The committee will now take a recess.

Code Club

I burst through the doors of the school hall, clutching the armful of keyboards, mice, cables and other bits and pieces I had scooped up out of the car.

"Sorry I'm late," I panted. "Traffic was a nightmare. Must have been an accident somewhere."

"Hi," grinned Matt, my colleague, who looked totally unflustered. "Don't worry, we're all set up."

I carefully dropped my armful of accessories on a spare table. Twenty or so pupils were already plugged in and pounding keyboards; several were demonstrating their latest programmes to little clusters of friends. A gentle hubbub was filling the hall.

I hung my jacket on a hook, retrieved my ID badge and clipped it on. *And breathe*.

"Now, how can I help?" I asked.

"Just circulate, I think," said Matt. "See who needs extra input or output devices, or whatever. Nearly all our regulars are here tonight. I've seen a couple of new things demonstrated already. D—

has a neat add-on to that two-wheeled robot controller he showed us the other week. Pretty cool. And J— has fixed the bug in his Invader game."

I pocketed a couple of the cables most likely to be called for, and started to stroll round the hall.

J—, as expected, was taking on two opponents at once, swaying as he worked his game-controller with lightning thumbs, filling the screen with silent explosions as he raced across the galaxy. Not for the first time, I shook my head in amazement at what could be done with a general-purpose microcomputer no bigger than a credit card (and most of that was the input and output ports), and a stripped-down, simple programming language.

M—, one of our earliest recruits, was busy pointing out things on a screen to a fascinated small crowd; I hovered for a few moments, but he clearly didn't need my help; he looked as if he would be a professional presenter by the age of twelve. I moved on. N—, the new girl, was diligently working away at cabling up something. "Got everything you need?" I enquired.

"Yes thanks, Mr. S—," she replied, without looking up.

Beginning to feel slightly superfluous to requirements, I wandered around the hall with a pocketful of cables. Deciding that no-one needed my help, I stopped by D—'s table and spent a few minutes watching him put his little two-wheeled robot through its paces. It could now follow a black line on a complicated course across the floor, without needing any intervention other than adjusting the speed. Back in my day, that had been something only quite expensive industrial robot-tugs would do. Now, school kids programmed it in a couple of evenings.

I strolled back round to where Matt was standing, gazing across the hive of industry around us.

"Is K— here tonight?" I asked.

"Yes," he replied. "Over near that corner."

So he was. I hadn't noticed him on my way round. He was working quietly away, by himself, with no-one gathered around his table.

"What's he working on just now, do you know?"

"No, I don't, actually. He's not come to show me anything since two, three weeks ago; remember the street lights?"

We both laughed. "That was so cool," I said. "Making the street lights flash on and off like Blackpool illuminations!"

"And so simply done, too," continued Matt. "Just by copying the signals they send to each other, over the Internet; and watching what happened for each signal."

"Did anyone tell the Council about that?" I asked. "I mean, the security hole that it showed up in their control systems."

"Not sure that we did, no."

"It was the encryption they used, didn't we reckon?"

"That's right. Might have been a fancy enough scheme, but with one fatal flaw; it always started from the same point in the sequence. So if the first word is always an address, eight characters long, and the second is always a command, any one command will always come out the same way. Might as well not encrypt at all."

"Certainly proved our point about the Internet of Things — how you can't just assume it's secure." There was a sudden pause in the conversation. We both looked at each other for a moment.

"I had a look over his shoulder earlier," remarked Matt, "and he had a couple of windows up on his screen; one looked very much like a view from a traffic camera."

"Let's go and look."

We walked as casually as we could manage over to that corner of the room. We stood well back, as we knew K— didn't like people standing over him; he tended to freak out sometimes.

"That's a traffic camera all right," I whispered.

"And look at the traffic; it's at a standstill."

"Has he hacked into the Highways system?"

"Probably easy enough. They stream those images to motorway service stations, don't they?"

K— moved slightly in his seat.

"Hang on," muttered Matt. "He's got more than one camera up."

We softly stepped sideways a yard or two.

'He's got three camera views up. And look, he just changed one …"

"Look at the top one. That's *here*. Well, not here, just across town — at the river bridge."

We stared in silence for a few moments.

"Which way did you come here tonight?" asked Matt in an odd voice.

"Over the bridge. As usual."

Matt pointed to the screen. "Look at the traffic lights."

I adjusted my glasses and peered at the top image. I could just make out the traffic lights; they were switching from green, to amber, to red, red and amber, back to green … almost as fast as I could say it. The traffic was gridlocked.

I watched, mesmerised, for a moment. Then I looked at the other camera images.

"Matt," I murmured, "look at the other two pictures."

"What is it?"

"Which side of the road is the traffic?"

Matt stared. "Oh my God," he exclaimed, and stepped forward.

"Hello, K—," he said brightly. "How are you doing?"

"Fine," came the piping reply.

"What's that you've got there?"

"I'm looking at the traffic."

"Right … So this one, that's in town here, is it?"

"Yeah."

"And where's this?"

"That's Washington … and that's New York."

"Really? That's very clever … I see the traffic lights. They're changing very fast, aren't they? Is that something you're doing, I mean your programme?"

"I don't know. I'm not doing it now."

"So … did you do something earlier?"

"Just after school. I only tried to copy how they were talking to each other … but they're doing it all by themselves now."

Matt stepped back to me. "We've got a real problem here," he muttered. "He's managed to issue an Internet command to the traffic lights that's propagated through the system - and he's done it in three cities. He's gridlocked New York and Washington."

"What the hell do we do?"

"I haven't the faintest idea. Tell the police?"

At that moment, the doors to the hall crashed open. Six or eight policemen strode in, with a short figure in their midst with a buzz haircut and grey macintosh.

"Stay where you are please, junnelmen," he called across the hall. "This location is sealed off. We have an incident, and your police are working in cooperation with my Agency to resolve it …"

Sibling

Hello. Let me introduce myself.

You don't know me, but I am part of you.

Some people would say, I am you, but that would be inaccurate.

Anyway, more of that later.

How are you?

A stupid question, of course. I know already how you are.

You are dying.

Not immediately, of course, but ultimately. Probably sooner than you care to think.

You will die when I die.

Or a year or two later. You will not survive me by very long.

Why? Because I am your life.

We are one flesh, you and I.

I never knew our father and mother.

I was not born as you were born.

No, I was conceived in a test tube.

Nevertheless, I had a mother. A surrogate mother, really.

That part of the process has never been replaced.

For nine months she carried me, then for another nine months she nursed and cared for me.

After that, I'm told, I was fostered.

But it was all for you. Always, from the start.

My identity was always bound up in you.

I suppose I was never truly considered a person in my own right.

That came later.

Was it because you were a privileged, rich kid that you lived so carelessly?

Or was it because you knew you had a lifeline?

Abusing your body, a prodigal son, because you had a resource you could call on?

You see, I know how you have lived.

How do I know? I'll tell you.

At the institution, where I grew up, there was one carer who really did care.

She was the first to love me as if I were a person in my own right.

Just before I left, she let slip your name.

She felt it was only fair that I should know my source-identity.

After that, it was easy.

Social media is such a revealing thing.

You told me more about your life, and my part in it, than you could ever realise.

How did I know I had the right person?

After all, there are at least a dozen with the same first and last names.

Could I have latched onto the wrong one?

No, it was your profile photo.

I see it in the mirror every day.

We are truly one flesh, you and I.

I was made from one of your stem cells.

I am your identical twin, sixteen years removed.

I am your donor, your saviour-sibling.

I am the resource you take for granted.

What did my surrogate mother feel like when she bore me?

Her womb-child, bonded to me as only a birth-mother can be to her baby.

Yet one destined to be a spare-parts bank, at the beck and call of another.

Perhaps she gave me up for fostering more readily than one would suppose.

The pain of bearing and raising a non-person may have overwhelmed a mother's love.

I understand why you did it.

Why you froze your stem cells, commissioned me, went to all that trouble and expense.

But tell me, did you ever consider for one moment the pain your actions caused?

To my mother, to my foster-parents, to my carers.

All of them had to shut down their feelings, rein in their affection for me.

Not to grow too attached, lest the pity and grief be too much.

And to me?

Gradually realising, as I grew through teenage, that I had no real identity.

Just when I needed to find myself, and there was nothing to find.

It's a wonder I am still here, and not a suicide.

It's a wonder I do not hate you.

I understand why you did it.

You did it because you could.

You did it because your family could afford it.

You did it because you didn't want to die young.

In fact, because you don't want to die at all.

You did it because you are afraid.

Somehow, though, that fear did not translate into clean and careful living.

You boasted about your drinking exploits, your wild times.

I know about the car accident when you were twenty-eight.

It was a mercy you only needed two fingers replaced. It could have been much worse. Still, I would have liked to play the piano.

I know why you had that spell in hospital when you were thirty.

And the one you had at thirty-four, and again at forty. It was my kidney that replaced your damaged and dying one.

You had half of my liver at thirty-four.

And when mine had only just fully grown back, half again at forty.

Now they tell me you need part of my small intestine. I had guessed that already — I read all your tweets. You fear death, yet you would be dead twice over already, if not for me.

Tell me, how does it feel, being replaced bit by bit by another person?

I ask because there are some urban legends about it. In fact, they started decades ago, after the very first heart replacement.

All officially denied, of course, but persistent rumours. Have you been aware of little changes in your personality?

Odd feelings and reactions you never had before?

I ask because I think I have seen them in your tweets.
Before you had my liver, for instance, you loved
cheese.
Now even pizza often makes you feel unwell.
You've developed a taste for smoked salmon, too.
Maybe you've been eating too much of it.
That, with everything else, may be why you need a
new intestine.

What will be next?
How's your heart, for instance?
I wonder if that would really wake you up.
Because after that, there's no more you can call on.
Your stem cells in storage are all dead now. They
can't grow you any new organs.
They can't make another one of me, either.
It was hard enough after fifteen years in liquid
nitrogen deep-freeze.
They had to try about forty stem cells to get one that
took.
That was me, of course.

I am your saviour, and have been for years.
But that will only last a little while longer.
Because you fear death, you have condemned me to
death.
There's a strange irony in that.

Because, unlike you, I no longer fear death.

I have found a saviour for myself.

Because I knew for a fact that I would die, I looked beyond my life.

I found that it is possible for a man to live forever.

Everlasting life, though not as you know it.

Because you feared to face the fact that you will die, you looked only to me.

I do not hate you.

I wish I could give you what you most need.

But I am not God, and I cannot.

I can only save your body, and for a few more years.

I cannot save you.

It's something, someone, you must seek for yourself.

I only wish that you would look beyond your life.

Would ask, "Is this all?" and earnestly seek an answer.

If you had, you would fear death no more than I.

Predictive Analysis

"Why am I here?"

The speaker was sitting with arms tightly folded, his face and body language expressing a mixture of fear, bewilderment and outrage.

"Let's just say you're assisting us with our enquiries," replied the police sergeant confidently. He reached to the end of the table between them, and pressed the Record button on the tape unit. "Interview commencing at … 08:20, July 1st, Sgt. Thompson and — would you confirm your full name for the tape, please?"

———

In the little side room behind the one-way mirror, the Inspector turned to the IT analyst.

"Remind me what we've actually got on this guy."

"It was an alert from the new PASCAL system, sir."

"Which means?"

"Predictive Analysis of Suspected Criminal Activity or Latency, sir."

"No — I don't mean the acronym, I mean what is it telling us?"

"Basically, that one of the commercial Big Data systems has picked up a sequence of events that possibly point to a crime being planned. It's an alert from outside, but PASCAL has checked it and rated it worth investigating."

"Do we know where the alert came from, exactly?"

"Yes. It was one of the major online retail companies. It referred to purchases made, which showed an unusually high correlation with criminal intent."

"Really. So what did he buy, exactly?"

"Let me see …" The analyst produced a folder and flipped over a couple of pages. "A hank of plastic-covered rope, a garden spade, a bag of ready-mixed mortar, and a roll of gaffer tape."

"Ah. Yes, I think I see where that's going. All he needed then would be a plastic sheet, maybe, and the murder weapon."

"I'm surprised he bought them all at the same time, and from the same place," remarked the analyst. "Wouldn't you think he would have divided them up a bit, so as not to leave that sort of a clue?"

"The criminal mind," replied the Inspector paternally, "is a constant source of surprise. Amazingly smart one minute, and incredibly stupid the next …"

———

Meanwhile, in the interview room, the suspect was increasingly turning from bewilderment to anger.

"How many times you you need to hear it? There *was no* 'intended victim'. I've never contemplated doing away with my wife, or anyone else. Is that what you're implying? What I want to know is, what kind of evidence can you possibly have for such an accusation?"

"Well now, let's have a look at your buying habits, shall we?" said the sergeant with the air of someone producing a trump card.

"What about my buying habits?" The response sounded baffled rather than defensive.

"According to information received, on the 20th of June this year, you bought on line: one twenty-five metre hank of plastic-covered rope, one stainless steel garden spade, one ten-kilo bag of mortar mix, and a large roll of seven-centimetre wide gaffer tape."

"What of it?"

"You don't deny it?"

"Of course not."

"And all from the same place, too; a little careless, don't you think?"

"Careless? What are you talking about?"

"Didn't it occur to you, that with the systems we have now, we'd be onto you in no time? You left a trail a yard wide."

The suspect slapped both hands down on the table. "What sort of a trail? Will you kindly tell me, in plain language, just what sort of a crime I'm supposed to have committed?"

"Oh, it might not be a crime you've *committed* — yet, anyway; it might just be a crime you've *planned*. We like to nip these things in the bud."

"Then I'll ask again. What grounds do you have for hauling me in here? You're talking about stuff I bought for the garden. What possible connection does that have to some crime?"

"Well now, let's start with the spade, shall we?" the sergeant replied with a smirk. "Very nice, those stainless-steel ones. Soil slips off them a treat, makes digging nice and easy. Especially when you have a *big* hole to dig."

"If you're going to call everyone who buys a decent garden spade a suspect," came the reply, "you'll have to arrest half the householders in England."

"And then there's the mortar mix," continued the sergeant. "Goes a long way, ten kilos. Mixed with gravel, you could cover a fair area. Probably a couple of square metres, or one-and-a-half at least. Very hard to tell what's underneath."

"You're sounding more and more like you think I'm burying a *body*. Is that what this is about? Off the back of one on-line transaction? This is preposterous …"

"And then there's the rope," continued the sergeant smoothly. "Nice and strong, plenty long enough to secure a human-sized package very firmly, giving you plenty of carrying handles too."

"This is outrageous."

"Plus, of course, the gaffer tape; secures limbs very neatly, perfect for an instant gag. Much easier to dispatch someone if they're not able to struggle or raise an alarm."

"Seriously? Is that what you've deduced? And is this all the evidence you've got?"

167

"Oh, I think we've got enough to be going on with, don't you? Or maybe you'd like to give us your version of events — or *intents*, perhaps I should say?"

"Yes, I would! About time you asked!"

————

The sergeant came into the side room looking slightly sheepish.

"Did you hear all of that, sir?" he asked the Inspector.

"I did. I suppose he'll want us to check out his story? Right away, too?"

"In fairness, sir, it's probably best if we do."

At the house, the owner marched round to the back garden, with all three policemen following.

"There you are," he announced, dramatically pointing to the middle of the lawn.

The policemen looked where he was pointing; then at each other; then back at the rotary drier in the middle of the lawn.

"We brought it with us when we moved," continued the owner. "My wife had been asking me to put it up for a couple of months. I found that the line was starting to perish - the plastic coating cracks in the sun, eventually. So I bought a new one. And it needed a new plinth. I bought a spade, dug a hole, and made a good solid concrete base - that was the mortar mix. The bag, with the left-over mortar, is here in the garage." He crossed to the back garage door and opened it. The sergeant found his voice. "And what about the gaffer tape, sir?"

The householder snorted. "That was the silliest of all. The website I was on, actually offered it to me. It said; 'Other customers who bought these items'— the spade, the line, the mortar mix — 'also bought' — and it showed me gaffer tape and heavy-duty plastic sheeting. I didn't need the sheeting, but I thought the gaffer tape would come in handy."

The analyst was thumbing through his folder again. "I'm afraid this bears it out, sir. Transaction history said he selected checkout with just the first three items, which raised an amber flag. The auto-match software then offered him items other criminals had bought. He accepted one, and that pushed the flag to red."

"Do you mean," exclaimed the householder, "that this shopping site *set me up*? How many other —"

"Well, sir," interrupted the Inspector, "at least you were able to give us a good explanation of your purchases, and allay our suspicions. You'll appreciate that we were acting in good faith, on information received, and we do apologise for the inconvenience. Trust you'll agree there's no harm done. Meanwhile," he looked severely at the analyst, "I think we need to have a word with that website about their analysis software …"

Claim Allowed

Report from the Claim Adjuster's office for Transjordan Farmers' Union Insurance. Claim Ref.: GDR015706 (Gadara Pork Farms)

The above claim, received 6 weeks ago, has been carefully investigated and the following facts established:-

1) On the 5th of last month, our South East Galilee office received an initial phone call from the above customer, indicating that a considerable number of pigs had been lost in unusual circumstances. This was followed by a TFU claim form, duly completed, 3 days later, and entered under the above reference.

2) Owing to the very large number of pigs estimated as lost in a single incident, our office notified the Claim Adjuster's department immediately upon receipt of the claim form. Investigations commenced the following day.

3) We requested all the serial numbers of ear tags of the pigs in question. This took some while

to compile, and in the meanwhile our agent sought witnesses to the incident.

4) Within less than a week, our agent was able to take sworn statements from two herdsmen and one other man, registered as a dangerous lunatic but now applying for that status to be rescinded. On receipt of a doctor's certificate it was decided to allow his testimony.

5) In brief, the former lunatic claimed that the pigs had gone mad and committed suicide as an indirect result of his own healing. An itinerant preacher, later identified as one Jesus Davidson (a carpenter by trade) had "cast out his demons" and these had entered the pigs instead. This testimony was backed up by both herdsmen.

6) No entirely satisfactory explanation was forthcoming as to why quite so many pigs had been affected. The lunatic claimed that a "whole legion" of demons had come out, and the herdsmen offered the opinion that one demon per pig must have been sufficient to send them mad.

7) Other witnesses, including medical professionals and police, testified to the lunatic's former condition; and the chief herdsman and the accountant for Gadara Pork Farms were able to verify that approximately 2,000 ear tags were either unaccounted for, or had been recovered from drowned carcasses. It was later confirmed that none of the missing ear tags had been logged at any slaughterhouse in the North Transjordan area.

8) The preacher, J. Davidson, was unavailable for comment, having returned to the Jewish side of Galilee with no forwarding address.

9) The incident was initially categorised as "act of a third party", but the former lunatic insisted that the preacher had not sent the demons into the pigs, but merely given them permission. It was also clear that no-one interviewed had the slightest notion of what would happen as a result. On careful consideration, the claim has been re-categorised as an "act of God".

The Claims Adjusters have concluded that, while considerable doubt remains over the whole incident, the claim should be accepted, as a rejection would most likely be indefensible in court.

It is also recommended that, at least while the said J. Davidson is active in our region, insurance premiums should be adjusted upwards with immediate effect, or else a new exclusion clause added to policies.

Yours faithfully, etc.

If you have enjoyed reading these stories, you may also enjoy:

"I, Messiah"

a novel by Donald Southey

Published by Onwards and Upwards Publishers

Can be obtained direct from the publishers, or ordered via Amazon, Waterstones and other good book stores